About

Charlie was born in Colchester in 1999, the youngest of three sons. He then slid over the border and grew up in a variety of different rural Suffolk villages. In the years between leaving school and heading off to the Oxford School of Drama, he acted as one of his grandad's primary carers. Since graduating, he has written and performed both stand-up comedy and sketch comedy as one half of the duo fondly known as *The Burger Boys*. This is his writing debut.

The Mystery of Warren's Walk

Charlie Shephard

The Mystery of Warren's Walk

Vanguard Press

VANGUARD PAPERBACK

© Copyright 2024
Charlie Shephard

The right of Charlie Shephard to be identified as author of this work has been asserted by him in accordance with the Copyright, Designs and Patents Act 1988.

All Rights Reserved

No reproduction, copy or transmission of this publication may be made without written permission.
No paragraph of this publication may be reproduced, copied or transmitted save with the written permission of the publisher, or in accordance with the provisions of the Copyright Act 1956 (as amended).

Any person who commits any unauthorised act in relation to this publication may be liable to criminal prosecution and civil claims for damages.

A CIP catalogue record for this title is available from the British Library.

ISBN 978-1-83794-422-4

This is a work of fiction. Names, characters, businesses, places, events and incidents are either the products of the author's imagination or used in a fictitious manner. Any resemblance to actual persons, living or dead, or actual events is purely coincidental.

Vanguard Press is an imprint of
Pegasus Elliot Mackenzie Publishers Ltd.
www.pegasuspublishers.com

First Published in 2024

Vanguard Press
Sheraton House Castle Park
Cambridge England

Printed & Bound in Great Britain

Dedication

For my darling Liv, the Lillian to my Desmond. Also, for John, a Desmond, if ever there was one.

Acknowledgements

Thank you to Grandma and Grandad, without whom this story wouldn't exist. Thank you to Mum, Dad, Will and George for moulding me into the kind of person who finds both ecstasy and solace in writing stories. Thank you to Sarah Mason for her support and encouragement, both in the fictional world of Orsworth and in our real one. Thank you to Stella and Caitlin for being the first to see Des' tale through to the end and for your kind words. Thank you to Luke, "Lovely Luke", whose sense of humour and coquettish smile are both undying lights in the darkness. Thank you to everyone at Pegasus Publishers for taking a punt on a young cardigan enthusiast such as myself. Thank you to everyone who thought that the village of Orsworth and its residents deserved exploring. And finally, thank you to Liv for being a constant source of joy and happiness.

Introduction

It's the end of 2014, a year that has seen an awful lot of unexpected twists and turns: *Birds of a Feather* revived on ITV, the word "vape" crowned Oxford Dictionary's word of the year, and the Sheffield Half Marathon cancelled due to a lack of water supplies for runners on the route. One thing that perhaps nobody in this year of the horse could've predicted is that in nine years' time, a young man, wearing nowt but his Merrimac memory foam moccasin slippers and a wry smile, will write a tale set in this very real year. The story itself will be based upon an entirely fictional village in East Anglia, Orsworth, finding its home just north of the Dedham Vale. Orsworth is frequently rumoured to be haunted; however, no proof has ever been found in support of this suspicion, until now.

It is time, dear reader, to fasten your seatbelt, check your blind spot, and straighten your varifocals because you and I are going to safely drive headfirst into the village of Orsworth together. Perhaps we're listening to Radio 2, or maybe you're happy with the sound of birds in trees and the slow grinding noise of metal on metal as my brake pads cease to perform their necessary function. Either way, one thing is for sure, we're entering this story as a team, hand in hand. I mean, my hands are most likely on both the wheel and the gearstick of the 2004 Renault Clio I'm driving, but let's not get bogged down in the murky depths of detail; let's just ruddy get on with it.

**Welcome to Orsworth
Please Drive Carefully Through Our
Village**

Chapter One
Saturday 13 December

Desmond Featherby was a delightful old codger and the proud owner of a spectacularly bald head, which was so smooth it made a Clarence Court free-range egg look like a young Kurt Cobain. He was chipper and cheeky in his youth and charming in his old age. If you are picturing an aged Gregg Wallace, you're on the right lines. For the past nine years since the passing of his late lady wife, Desmond had kept himself company, as they had been unsuccessful when it came to the conception of offspring. However, they had adopted several cocker spaniels in their time, which in Desmond's words, were "more or less the same". Desmond was eighty-four years young. He lived in a bungalow with Jarvis, the cocker. Jarvis was an elderly spaniel, made up of ears that barely functioned, eyes that just about saw, and a hunger for anything and everything besides the branded dog food Desmond bought for him.

It was a frosty Saturday morning. 13 December 2014, to be specific, 8:37 a.m., if you were at all curious. Two figures were crunching the leaves beneath their feet as they trod their well-trodden morning route. Of course it was our pensioner protagonist, Desmond, plodding along with Jarvis by his side, when suddenly he bolted. Jarvis, that is, not Desmond; Desmond hasn't bolted anything of late, besides the front door, to keep those pesky youths at bay. No, no, it was Jarvis, he'd picked up the scent of something in the woodland up ahead. Despite having the eyes and ears of a homemade ceramic teapot, he had the nose of an incredibly youthful and slender bloodhound. Desmond called after the dog, 'Jarvis, come back here, old boy!' and he gave a whistle through his dentures, the sort of whistle that only men above the age of sixty-eight seem to be able to master. Jarvis did not return. 'Right, so we're playing that game then, are we?' Desmond muttered to himself as he trudged up the bridle path leading into the trees.

Desmond, or Des as his friends called him, I say "called" because Desmond only had two friends in the village, and neither were around anymore. One being his lady wife, Lillian, and the other, his old drinking pal, Brian. Sadly, as we discussed, Lillian passed away nearly a decade ago and Brian, well, after a spout of falls, angry outbursts, and one incident involving a shoehorn and a NutriBullet, Brian's daughters had decided to move him into a nursing home. So, it was just Des and Jarvis, and now Jarvis seems to have buggered off.

Desmond's unsteady feet trod a winding path through the wood. The public footpath that was supposedly meant to be signposted had long been lost to the falling of autumn leaves and the maze-like tyre tracks that those young boys in their hoods had made with their BMXs and other cycles. As Des staggered his way through the foliage, calling out for Jarvis as he went, he heard movement up ahead. Unlike Jarvis, Des had excellent hearing thanks to his Widex Clear 440 hearing aids, a treat from Des to Des on his 80th birthday. The noise he had detected seemed to be a rustling, it appeared to be coming from a den made up of branches and well, more branches. Jarvis had likely found a wrapper of some sort, or even better, a full packet of BBQ Beef flavoured Hula Hoops still sealed, they were Jarvis' favourite. As Des approached the den, the rustling stopped, then it started again, this time it was off to the right behind a gnarled hornbeam. 'That bloody dog, what's he up to now?' Des mumbled to himself as he slowly rotated 30 degrees to face the new source of sound. He took three steps forward. The sound stopped. Des stood still, he whistled one last time, and then he fell. Desmond Edmund Featherby fell, despite having never taken a step.

Falling in what felt like slow motion, Des saw Lillian emerge from behind the tree, wearing nothing but a white dress and a giddy smile, barefooted, she stumbled graciously towards him, reaching out her hand, then quick as a flash she faded away, only to be replaced by his father, beaming with pride as he wrung Desmond's hand, no sooner had the handshake settled into a comfortable rhythm then the image changed yet again, this time it was Brian, leaning over the snooker table that had just risen up from the frosted earth, Des watched as Brian missed his shot, knowing that Brian would hand him the cue and Des would pot the black, bouncing it off the side, into the middle pocket, the one closest to the gents. Sure enough, he watched the whole thing play out before his eyes, the first and only time he ever beat Brian at snooker. Brian grinned and walked away, dragging the table with him as he went, the trees were also uprooting themselves and leaving Des behind, he followed them with his gaze until nothing remained, not even darkness itself, and that is when his head hit the ground.

Chapter Two
Saturday 13 December

'The body of Desmond Featherby, resident of Honeycomb Cottage, Queensbury Close, was found this morning by a couple of doggers. From now until further notice, the woodland, known locally as Warren's Walk, has been cordoned off by the local Police Constabulary.'
Extract from the *Orsworth Evening Gazette*.

Desmond's skull made contact with the earth; he lay still for all of thirty seconds. It was the shuffling of footsteps which brought Des to his senses. After opening his eyes, he quickly staggered to his feet, surprisingly quickly for a man with two hip replacements and a tendency for headrush. Jarvis had come bounding over, having given up on the squirrel he had sniffed out, it had eluded him by climbing up a silver birch, always an unfair tactic, regardless of the tree species.

Jarvis began to bark rather incessantly. Des responded as he always had, 'Calm down, ye daft dog.' The barking continued, Des looked around to see where Jarvis was so he could pat his head to quieten him down, but then his eyes locked onto the thing that Jarvis was barking at. It was

Des. There was another Des lying on the ground where he, Des had just fallen.

Des blinked several times so as to make sure what he was seeing wasn't some sort of horrible hallucination, the kind that one might have during a seriously bad trip after taking some psilocybe cubensis or any other variety of psychedelic mushroom. Des only knew of psilocybe cubensis because Brian had shown him an article all about the health benefits of "magic fungi" on the webpage *www.shroomformore.co.uk*. Des was not convinced, he was firmly of the belief that if you had a glass of cow's milk before bed every night, none of this oat and nut nonsense, then you would be absolutely fine. Yet here he was, the opposite of absolutely fine, absolutely dead in fact. And what's more, he hadn't had his gold top last night, as he'd had to use more milk the previous morning, thanks to Jarvis spilling his entire bowl of Rice Krispies Multigrain Shapes.

Mushrooms and milk aside. This was no drug experience, this was real. Real weird for sure, no doubt, but still very much real. There he was on the ground and also, here he was standing upright. Des noticed a large rock, some might contest that it was a small boulder, but Des estimated it to be a large rock. The rock was stained with blood. His blood. As he reached out to pick up the rock, he noticed his hands weren't covered in his dog walking gloves, Lillian's last Christmas present to him, a nice pair of racing green Joules Bamburgh gloves.

Lillian's friend, Verity, had a daughter, Annie, who worked at Joules at the time, and she gave Lillian her twenty-five per cent discount. Lillian utilised this connection every Christmas, to the point at which one might say she was "taking the Michael". Des never said this; however, he always opened his present, smiled, and said, 'Thank ye, darlin', that's right, nice that is,' before handing over his present, some knick-knack that he'd knocked up in his shed. Past presents included, a neat, wooden plant pot, a pair of scrabble tile holders, and on one occasion, a hastily made rolling pin which Lillian mistook for a log and promptly chucked on the fire. Des didn't tell her what she had done and instead nipped out to the shed and cobbled together a frame, into which he slipped the photograph of the two of them running the tombola stall at the 1999 Village Fete. *A good save*, Des thought.

Des looked down, not only was he without his gloves, but he was also without anything else. He was stark-bollock naked, not a stitch on him, not even his spotted Wellington boots, also from Joules. Des immediately covered up his gentleman's agreement, which he wasn't ashamed to admit took both of his rather large hands to hide, despite the cold. Yet, it wasn't cold, despite it being near Baltic when he left the house, Des was now at what he would describe, "a rather mild temperature". Jarvis was still barking away at the fully clothed and fully gloved body on the ground, Des had given up trying to quieten him.

There was a sudden rush of footsteps, two young women had come hurrying into the woods, both wearing luminescent headbands and wrapped up in matching black and yellow striped jackets. Des was immediately reminded of Beequiet and Beehave, the two bumblebees from *Stoppit and Tidyup*, the BBC children's animation which first aired in 1988 and really should have had a longer shelf life than it did, in Desmond's opinion. You may be wondering why Des, a childless man in his 50s at the time, was watching the latest children's television. Well, the simple answer is, he did not know how to change the channel on his Sony Trinitron colour television without Lillian's help, and she was otherwise occupied.

The two women had followed the direction of Jarvis' barking. They stopped running, they both paused the "Outdoor Run" activity tracker on their respective Apple Watches, and then they saw Des, the lying-down Des, that is. The standing, naked Des was desperately trying to explain what had happened, how he had fallen, come to, got up and was now suddenly in the nude, which he was terribly apologetic about, but he honestly didn't know how it had occurred, he then tried to explain that he'd momentarily lost the dog and was following him but couldn't find him, but he thought he had heard him rustling about, but—

''Scuse me,' said Des, 'are you listening to a word I'm sayin'?' They weren't. The ladies were frantically searching their luminescent pockets for a mobile telephone. One of them, Henrietta (Des recognised her from the village pub quiz at The Common Inn, a rather ingenious pub name Des always thought), had found her device and was calling for the emergency services.

Chapter Three
Saturday 13 December

Two police officers arrived on the scene within minutes – seventeen minutes to be precise – PC Dunston and PC Bates. It was only a small village, and the local police department was a mere stone's throw away from Warren's Walk. Eric Dunston was both incredibly lanky and blessed with the reddest of hair, if I were to compare it to a Farrow & Ball shade it would be the perfect mixture of "Incarnadine" and "Charlotte's Locks". If PC Dunston were also in the nude, his slender frame and bright hair would be perfectly reminiscent of a lit match. Bates, on the other hand, was short and stocky. Their left arm was covered in a sleeve of individual tattoos, all of which had a deep, emotional resonance with Bates, but to the casual observer, it just looked like Bates was a huge fan of Marmite, rubber ducks, and Stephen King novels. The officers, who were talking to the witnesses, seemed totally oblivious to the bare-bottomed pensioner who stood hunched over the scene. They liaised with Henrietta and her friend, Lucy (Des overheard her give her name to the coppers). Des was getting frustrated. He had gone from scared to confused to panicked, back to confused via angry, bypassing a moment of madness when he began windmilling in the face of PC Dunston, right back to scared.

What the hell was going on?

Then came the arrival of local chief constable, Wendy Mack. Wendy was a friendly face around the village, her gentle Glaswegian accent was always a sign of comfort to those in need. She has been in the position for nearly three years, after her and her husband moved down from Norfolk, where she had been a lower-ranking police officer. In the short amount of time she has been in charge, she has cracked down on antisocial behaviour, vandalism and disorderly conduct, all by simply asking Gwendolene Channon to leave the Women's Institute, as she was a bad influence. Des liked Wendy, she always gave him a smile whenever they passed one another in Budgens. On one occasion, she helped him pick up a bag of cashews he had dropped by the tills. She would sort this out, stamp some authority on the situation. She entered the scene and clapped her rather large, Scottish hands together.

'Right, Dunston, fill me in.'

Dunston was a rather nervous and fretful officer, intimidated by Mack's prowess and stature, Mack knew this, and rather enjoyed the dynamic. 'Well, ma'am, these two young ladies say they heard a dog barking.'

'So, they called the police because a dog was barking?'

'No, ma'am, not quite.'

'Then cut to the chase.'

'Yes, ma'am, well, this is the dog that was barking.'

'You quite sure? Adamant that it's that dog, the only dog in the entire vicinity?

'I think so, ma'am, and, um... judging by her collar, she's called Lillian.'

'Do you really think a dog with cocks and balls that size is going to be called Lillian?'

'Sorry, ma'am?'

'That is evidently the owner's name, you incredulous buffoon. Now, if you'd like to stop talking about dogs and collars and perhaps fast forward to the body that is lying at our feet?'

Desmond was seeing and hearing all of this, where was the sweet lady who had winked at him in the bakery after she'd helpfully grabbed his buns?

Chief Constable Mack was now speaking to Henrietta and Lucy, leaving Dunston to mop his sweating brow with his uncle's ancient handkerchief.

'Now, I don't doubt this came as quite the shock. If you need anyone to talk to, then please pop by the station. We'll be in touch if we need anything more from you. As far as I'm concerned, you two should go home, pop the kettle on, and have a nice, restful day by the fire. Oh, and if you would not mind taking care of the dog, just until we see if this poor gentleman had any requests for who should look after him?' Mack asked in the kindest manner possible before she knelt down beside Des' corpse, retrieved the dog lead from around his neck, and gave it to Lucy.

'Of course, thank you,' Henrietta said. Lucy attached the lead to Jarvis' collar, the two women clasped hands and tried to make tracks. But Jarvis didn't want to go. He wanted to stay with Des. After putting up one hell of a struggle Jarvis lay down nestling into the crook of his deceased owner's arm. He started pawing at Des' hand, sniffing at his fingers, longing for the motionless limb to come to life and give him a pat or ruffle his ears. Henrietta picked Jarvis up, held him in her arms and journeyed home, with Jarvis looking over her shoulder and whining every step of the way.

Des, still stunned in silence, watched his best friend be taken away, while the officers taped off the area surrounding his body.

'First time?' came a voice.

Des near shit himself. He spun round with surprising speed, so fast in fact that it took a second or two for his above average sized phallus to stop swinging, rather like a spring door stop when you twang it. Only it wasn't a spring door stop, it was an old man's member.

The person who had spoken was standing right in front of him. She was much younger than Des, but her energy was that of an incredibly old soul. She too, was as naked as the day her mother birthed her, the only thing blemishing her skin was a thin line traced across her neck. Des stood speechless.

She asked again, 'First time?'

In that moment, Des suddenly realised that this was the first lady he'd seen naked since Lillian. His hands instinctively went back to cover up his piece of pork, lest it rear its head in curiosity.

'Oh, I wouldn't worry about that,' said the naked stranger. 'They don't work anymore, trust me.'

After another twenty seconds of silence and staring, she said, 'You're dead, dear. Your spirit has left your physical form and you have joined the rest of us. The rest of us who linger in this "in between" plane of existence.'

'Right... You – What...? How – Um...' Des stuttered.

'Oh goodness me, get your words out, man, come on, come on.' She was brisk and firm with Des, she spoke with an incredibly clipped tone. One might've thought her an excellently ruthless lawyer or a rather unapproachable paediatrician.

'What?'

'Perhaps I should be more plain. You're not at rest, and you're not eternally damned. It is nothing which you have done, don't worry or panic, it is simply because you were murdered.'

'What do you mean, m... m... murdered?'

'It's when someone kills someone else. Catch up. You were murdered, unjustly so, hence your prolonged existence. Now, we all know that the local authorities will brush this under the rug. Another old boy takes a tumble on an uneven footpath, it doesn't suggest there would be any foul play.'

'But, sorry, I don't understand, I was murdered? Who murdered me?'

'Whom, dear?'

'Actually, I think it is who in this case.'

'Is it? I'm not sure.'

'As in… you're not sure if it is who or whom, or you're not sure who murdered me?'

'Both, I suppose.'

'Bugger.'

'Yes. Bugger, indeed.'

There was silence.

'I am terribly sorry; I never asked your name?'

'Abigail.'

'Lovely name that, named after your mother or grandmother?'

'Neither. My mother's midwife had an unrecognisable Irish accent and when I was born, she said, "she's a big girl", and my mother misheard her and was so delirious at the time she just went along with it.'

'Oh right, well, it is a lovely name all the same. I'm Desmond.'

'Pleasure. Well Des, may I call you Des?'

'You may.'

'Well, while we've been exchanging pleasantries, Des, your body has been removed by the uniformed folk. We are now very much alone in this wood.'

'What about Jarvis, I don't know where those ladies live, will I ever be able to see him again?'

Abigail didn't respond. She was looking over Des' shoulder and smiling.

'Three! Three dogs today!' came a rough, coarse voice. Desmond gave a start, shocked by the arrival of yet another stranger, turning he saw the newcomer approaching. A rather chipper young man was staggering gleefully towards them from the direction of the village. He had a scraggly beard, dirty blonde hair, and just the one arm. Des noticed that he was hauling a rather large cylindrical shaped something between his legs as he scampered, a Peter Piper to compete with his own perhaps. The man's upper half was riddled with what appeared to be several stab wounds, they were such a sight to behold that they somehow pulled focus from his heavily scabbed bottom half, his tarriwags look as if they'd had a heated scuffle with a Microplane cheese grater. Desmond also now realised that what he had assumed to be an overly large nether-rod was in fact the man's dismembered arm.

'Don't fret,' said Abigail, 'this is Orvyn, our Saxonic friend, he's all right, in every sense of the word.' She beamed to herself; she had been waiting centuries to share her wordplay.

'Oh yeah, don't you worry about me mate, I'm "armless me".' Orvyn laughed through a barely toothed mouth.

'Now, Orvyn, these dogs, you didn't by chance see a small dog with two women?' asked Abigail carefully.

'THREE dogs in total Abi, Three! It's going to be a good day!' Orvyn loved dogs. They were his second favourite animals; horses were his number one. 'I saw a great big brown boy in a garden down past the ale house,

I saw another sniffing one of the lampposts on the main street, small dog that one was but had a mother and son with it, human mother and son, you understand, and last one I saw was a small black and white fella with the softest looking ears being carried by lady! Carried, I tell you! I said the pooch has got four legs, let him use them! She didn't hear me of course.'

'And was that one—'

'That one was with two ladies. I saw them going into their house, they didn't look too happy. How could they not be happy with that furry little thing in their lives?' Orvyn really was an energetic creature, he made the Duracell bunny look like a very, very slow rabbit.

Des looked slightly relieved, as relieved as any recently murdered man could. Abigail continued the questioning on his behalf, 'Can you remember which road they lived on?'

'Certainly can!'

'Would you like to tell us?'

'Absolutely, they're on Fir Tree Lane! I remember because there's a big fir tree at the end of the lane.'

'Well done, dear, full marks. There you are Des, don't fret, we can wander that way later.'

'Thank you, Abigail, and thank you, Orvyn. Say Orvyn, if you're a Saxon then why don't you have a Germanic accent?' inquired Des, tilting his head slightly.

'Well, I did, but over the years it's changed somewhat. Abi and I have had several centuries together, and this village doesn't see a lot of tourism, so I haven't heard my old accent for well over a thousand years. People change, Des mate, get over it.'

Conversation somehow began to flow between the three spirits. It transpired that Orvyn had been killed by one of his fellow warriors, slaughtered as he slept. Amongst the chaos of battle, he never discovered the suspect, and he has dwelt in this quaint East Anglian village ever since. Abigail on the other hand, was a slightly more recent member of the "Unjustly Murdered Club". She was of royal heritage. Lady Abigail Catherine Warren was her living name. She was killed whilst holidaying in the countryside in the middle of the seventeenth century, a bold excursion for any royal during a time of civil unrest, civil war in fact. She was mugged and when she refused to hand over the necklace that lay around her throat, the mugger slit it. The mugger was cloaked and heavily hooded, so as such was never caught or identified. Abigail brushed the scar that still marked her neck, Des watched her curiously, as he did, he lifted his left hand to the back of his head, where he felt a significant dent in his otherwise structurally sound skull.

The name "Warren" rang a bell in Des' memory. He recalled back in his earlier years, being told by the estate agent who had shown him and Lillian round their rather roomy two bedroom bungalow, that the village's claim to fame was being the death place of a distant member of the royal family in the 1600s. Des assumed that it had been a less gruesome death, but alas, Lady Abigail did not pass away in her sleep surrounded by family. No, no. She had

had her oesophagus torn apart by a jagged bit of flint, and then her body robbed of her grandmother's jewellery. At the time Orvyn had tried to help her solve the mystery behind her killer, but alas, the suspect had fled the county. Abigail explained to Desmond that they were limited to boundaries of the village or town in which they had perished. She found this out herself as she had walked North out of Orsworth in pursuit of her killer and then as soon as she passed Lollingworth Road, she found herself walking into Orsworth from the South, just off Bridge Street.

The sun flitted in and out of view behind the winter clouds, like a mischievous child playing hide and seek. The naked whispers of life walked as they chatted and as it happened, they chatted as they walked, Abigail and Orvyn were bickering about this and that. The dynamic between the Saxon and the Stuart was similar to that of a brother and sister. Despite Orvyn being a touch older when he had died, Abigail took on the role of older sibling, thanks to her being both more responsible and she liked being in charge. Desmond was both sixty years their senior and yet centuries more inexperienced than them, so where he fits into this family dynamic, who can say? All we know is that Abigail and Orvyn liked Des, and they wanted to help him adjust to this new life, so they let him lead the group. Desmond was unconsciously guiding the trio back to his very own front door. Of course, everything he now did was unconscious, but that is neither here nor there.

They were just turning left into Queensbury Close when Desmond halted. He was looking up ahead. Staring solemnly at the sight that lay before him. Jarvis curled up on the porch, his head resting on the morning paper with two bottles of gold top next to him.

The girl who delivered the Orsworth Gazette was a sweet young thing, but it always got on Des' nerves that she could never be bothered to post the bloody paper, she always threw it somewhere near the front door. Once, after he had already sent a strongly worded letter to the newsagents about not receiving that morning's paper, he had found it, in amongst his Buddleia. Upon seeing Jarvis using it as a makeshift pillow, however, a wave of gratefulness for the young girl's laissez faire approach to her morning shift washed over him. He felt himself smile for the first time since he had died.

Chapter Four
Saturday 13 December

Henrietta and Lucy had evidently decided to leave Jarvis be for the time being, for neither of them were in sight. Des watched his old dog snoozing away for what felt like hours. He wasn't sure how long he'd stood there; time was a tricky ol' blighter in this realm. Seconds seemed to simultaneously trickle by and fly by. Several minutes or potentially hours later, Henrietta came striding round the corner, lead in one hand and a small handful of Cathedral's Extra Mature Cheddar in the other. Des smiled. Jarvis will be just fine. The spaniel's snout began to twitch as it picked up the scent, and soon enough, he was up on all fours wagging his tail, trotting on over to Henrietta. Des was glad that Jarvis was going to be well looked after. Although he did feel a slight pang of annoyance that all it had taken for his best friend to stop grieving was a small amount of cheese. But so be it. Jarvis was happy, so Des was happy.

Des' eyes went from the porch to the bungalow as a whole. His home for the last twenty-eight years. He took a step towards the front door, as he did so he heard a gentle cough from behind him.

'You won't be allowed in, I'm afraid, Desmond,' came Abigail's voice, slow and light.

'It's one of the rules. You can look but can't touch,' Orvyn added.

Desmond was mildly affronted. This was his home. If he wanted to go in, have a sit down and enjoy a slice of Annie's carrot cake, whilst flicking through Prue Leith's autobiography, then he bloody well will. He stumped on up to the front door and then realised he hadn't got his keys. They were in his coat pocket. His coat which was now probably in some sort of plastic sealed bag in Dedwich Hospital mortuary, along with his flamingo printed socks and, Des ached with embarrassment, his underpants. His holey underpants. By which I mean they were riddled with holes, they didn't have the nativity scene across the backside, or the ten commandments stitched into the waistband. That would be ridiculous. They were just holey. Full of holes. Seriously, the gusset looked like it had been host to a well-attended moth orgy. What made it worse was that these were the only holey pair of briefs that Desmond owned. His nice, John Lewis, cotton boxers were all still drying on the airer in the utility room.

'Note to self, always wash your clothes before it's too late,' Desmond uttered under his breath. Before realising that it was indeed too late. He was dead. Not just dead, but dead and naked. No need for pants, holey or otherwise. Desmond focussed himself. He just wanted to get into his house. He trudged round to the back door where the spare key was kept. He bent down to lift the plant pot which hid the key. He couldn't move it. He could not physically touch the pot. It was as if there were an impenetrable force field surrounding his Agapanthus. He stood up, frowning his brow and tapped his chin with his forefinger, thinking. He tried nudging the pot with his left foot, no luck. He tried his right foot, still no dice.

'Bugger.' Des exhaled.

He'd never wanted for much in his life and all he wanted in death was just to see the inside of his home one last time. To feel the sofa cushions, to hear the whistling of his kettle as it boiled. To see Lillian's picture that stood on his bedside. He began to panic that he'd forget what she looked like without it. How could he ever forget her face? Those hazel eyes, that button nose, he'd certainly never forget that scar on her chin from their 30th anniversary in London. They were both rather drunk and Lillian had challenged Des to a race across Westminster Bridge. The winner was never confirmed, because Lillian fell over trying to take off her shoes, hitting the floor chin first. A long night in A&E and several stitches later, she had a funny story to tell Verity when they got back home.

Abigail and Orvyn had appeared round the side of the house, just as the sun began to set beyond the horizon. They smiled at Des.

'It's hard to comprehend now, but you'll get used to it,' assured Abigail.

Des tried to smile in response but couldn't. Abigail elbowed Orvyn.

'Oh, yeah, umm, chin up pal. Why err, why don't you show us your favourite spots in the village, eh? That always cheers me up.'

Des hesitated. He looked at Honeycomb Cottage, a place once full of merriment and laughter but for the last nine years a place of solitude and a reminder of what once was. This had been his favourite spot in the village, his home, but he supposed there were other places of significance. He took a deep breath, turned, and nodded in response to Orvyn, like a child who had been asked if jelly and ice cream might make their tummy feel better.

He was dead. He was dead, and he was just about to take two ancient spirits for a personalised guided tour around the village. What a positively bizarre end to a rather gruesome and peculiar day.

Chapter Five
Saturday December 13

Des, Abigail and Orvyn, the three naked spirits, walked out of Queensbury Close, up Hungerford Avenue and onto the Highstreet. What would Beatrice Allen, head of both the Neighbourhood Watch and the Women's Institute, say if she looked out of her window and saw three totally nude ghosts strutting down the street. The youngest member of this ghoulish group was swinging his dismembered arm about like it was a rounders bat, all the while the old man's well sized genitals were swaying to and fro with every step he took. Poor old Beatrice would probably have a stroke. But alas, she couldn't see them as they passed her front door and continued up to the church. The gate to the church was open, it always was. The vicar was a forgetful lady. Once, she forgot how to finish a prayer. Imagine that, a member of the clergy forgetting the word "Amen", it was just a minute and a half of awkward silence before one of the community choir prompted her.

Desmond led his fellow spectres to the back corner of the graveyard, behind the church, where the footpath meets the bridleway leading to Warren's Walk.

Just past Simon Thorne, Verity's late husband, lay a beautiful, granite headstone which simply read:

Lillian Elizabeth Featherby
Born August 1938
Died October 2005
A loving wife and a loyal friend

'Here's my Lillian' – Des simpered – 'I come every morning, Jarvis and I sit on this tree stump here and I fill her in on what I've watched, anything from *Grand Designs* to *Naked Attraction*.'

'It's lovely, Des, it really is,' Abigail commented politely. Orvyn just smiled, nodding his head in agreement.

In silence, they walked round the back of the church, past a rather large plinth supporting an even larger cross. The most distinctive gravestone in the area by a country mile. The engraved letters had been completely lost to nearly four hundred years of weathering.

'This is me' – Abigail smiled – 'my parents were ashamed by my manner of death. Both my lady in waiting and the local priest had written to them, informing them of my passing. They didn't want my body brought back to London and nor did they want to attend my funeral. It was a small service, done in the dead of night so as not to draw attention. My lady in waiting and the priest were the only people in attendance. Orvyn and I were there also, bumping up the numbers.' Tears would've been trickling down Abigail's cheek, if her tear ducts had belonged to a living human being.

'I'm sorry to hear that. Did they ever come to visit, your parents?' asked Des.

'No. The last contact I ever had with them was reading their response to Reverend Cotwin's letter, in which they stated that they shan't ever travel North of Colfield. They made no mention of my name.' A short moment of silence followed, in which Des stared at Abigail, who was looking mournfully at the plinth. Abigail's eyes left her grave and found Desmond's gaze,

'You would think that after nearly four hundred years, talking about death would be easy. The fact is that when we die, those emotional wounds never quite heal. Those feelings, however raw, stay with you. We've just got to do what we can to manage.'

Des had, of course, experienced grief. He had grieved for Lillian, for his parents and for eight cocker spaniels. He'd never had to grieve for himself, however. It was odd, but if there was anyone that could help him through it, it was two people who had been doing it for centuries.

There came a clinking of bottles from just over the hedge next to where the three friends stood. They went out onto the road to see who was making such a noise at this time. It was Reverend Daniels, sneaking out of the vicarage in the dead of night to do her bottle run. The group of ghosts followed her down the street to the bottle bank in the Budgens car park.

They walked past Annie's bakery. Des had been in there only three days ago, buying a sumptuously moist carrot cake, Annie's best. Annie, if you remember, was

Verity's daughter. She left her job at Joules six years ago to help care for her father, Simon, who had vascular dementia. Sadly, Simon's condition rapidly deteriorated and he passed away, just two weeks before his 75th birthday, leaving Annie a rather handsome inheritance. Annie used this money to set up her bakery in what used to be a moderately unsuccessful chiropodist. The bakery struggled at first, but over the last four months or so, it had positively exploded with clientele. People coming and going, even people from outside of the village came to Orsworth for Annie's baked goods.

Des watched the vicar, painfully trying to quietly place her Trivento Malbec and Sipsmith's Gin into the mixed bottle bank. Reverend Daniels seemed to wince at the smashing of each bottle, whether that was due to an alcohol induced headache or concern about the amount of noise she was making, was unclear. What was clear was that this vicar did not want to be seen recycling her many empty bottles.

Suspicious? Perhaps.

Intriguing? Potentially.

A completely irrelevant piece of storytelling which deviates from the central plot? Maybe.

Des, Abigail and Orvyn had left. Walking back up the high street. Abigail was explaining the practicalities of nighttime as a ghost.

'People think ghosts haunt at night. It's ridiculous. You don't suddenly become nocturnal when you die, we need to rest, just like everybody else.'

'Right, so where do we sleep then?' asked Des, an understandable amount of anxiety in his voice.

'It's quite bleak, I'm afraid. You sleep where you ceased to exist,' said Abigail bluntly, 'so you and I are neighbours! I was killed only a hundred yards or so from where you were. Orvyn on the other hand... well, you'll see.'

The three of them walked along the high street, heading towards the edge of the village. They walked past Budgens with its Christmas lights twinkling in the front window, they stopped briefly to look at the post box outside the Post Office, which had a knitted Christmas Pudding atop it, no doubt Beatrice Allen's handy work and they were just going past the pelican crossing when the other two stopped. Des carried on walking and turned to ask Orvyn a question about Saxonic brewing methods before he realised that he and Abigail had stopped by the crossing. He hurried back to them.

'Home sweet home.' Orvyn grinned, looking into the middle of the road.

'I beg your pardon,' Des responded.

'This is me; this is where I "ceased to exist". Ploughed down by a Timothy Taylor's delivery truck I was,' Orvyn exclaimed dramatically.

'I thought you were brutally slaughtered in your sleep?' said Des.

'Thanks for the reminder. Can't a man dream of a more valiant death. Cheers, Desmondo,' grumbled Orvyn as he walked into the middle of the road, lay down on the tarmac, and cuddled his other arm, like a child would with a stuffed Paddington Bear toy or a comforting piece of muslin. Orvyn's snores began to fill the otherwise silent night.

'Come on. We better get some rest too, especially if we want to find out who is responsible for putting you here,' said Abigail wisely.

The two ghosts made their way back to Warren's Walk, Abigail dropped Des off by the trees where he had fallen earlier that day, police tape flapping in the wind, blood spattered rock still in place. He awkwardly lay down, as far from the rock as he could.

'Shut your eyes and you will enter a dreamless state. Don't worry, I'll stay until you doze off,' Lady Abigail hushed.

Des was fast asleep within seconds. It had been a long day after all.

Chapter Six
Sunday 14 December

Now, it has thus far taken us five chapters to cover one single day. If we're ever going to make it to Christmas and find out who on earth killed poor old Des, we're going to need to pick up the pace. From this moment henceforth, each chapter shall cover the events of one day, in chronological order of course, there's no need to add further confusion to a story which is already riddled with complications. If a chapter does not end with our protagonist and friends settling to rest, just assume they have, and it hasn't been documented. Now, let us dive headfirst back into the murky midst of this murder mystery. After you!

*

Desmond Featherby awoke after quite possibly the best sleep he'd ever had. No dreams to disturb his slumber, no midnight toilet trips, and Jarvis hadn't barked once. Bliss. Once his eyes had acclimatised to his surroundings however, that feeling of bliss had quite vanished. He was, of course, lying, quite naked, where we had left him.

Des propped himself up on his elbows, surveying his new sleeping quarters: plenty of frosty soil, an old bird's nest that must've fallen from a branch above, and rather suitably, a plentiful amount of decaying leaves. Near his feet there was a patch of earth that appeared dented, flatter than the ground around it. Almost as if someone else's head had rested there, creating the temporary image in Desmond's mind that he had been in an intimate position with someone in the night. A position that Des knew as somewhere between 68 and 70, a position that Urban Thesaurus tells me can also be called "fellatialingus", "chicken and broccoli" and, believe it or not, "need for speed most wanted". Desmond himself had never been quite so sexually experimental, he had, of course, learnt of this particular positioning from Brian and one of his websites. Des shrugged and then began grunting as he helped himself onto his feet. His pendulous privates swung back and forth as he rose.

Abigail was striding towards him, a smile on her face 'Someone is a late riser!'

'All right, how are ye?' mumbled Des.

'Very well, thank you. How did you sleep?'

'Actually, incredibly well as it goes,' Des replied, showing the early signs of a grin.

Abigail's eyes swept the floor. 'You've lucked out here, plenty of leaves and twigs, what more could you want?'

'You mean apart from being alive?'

'Well quite, but aside – hang on.' She was still surveying Des' sleeping quarters, 'Where's the rock?'

'Begging ye pardon?' Des yawned, stretching his arms to the sky as he did so.

'The rock. The rock that was here last night as you lay to rest, the same rock which was, forgive my brutishness, smattered in your blood.'

Des looked at the ground. She was absolutely right. Of course he hadn't been entwined in a "horizontal banana split" overnight, that flattened bit of earth was where the brain-stained rock had lain, and that rock was now missing. Where had it gone? Had someone come and removed it? If so, did they take it in the dead of night, or first thing this morning? As Des' mind raced with these questions, he also noticed that the police tape that had been flapping last night had been fixed more securely to the surrounding yew trees. Someone had definitely been creeping around here while he slept.

'Let's go and find Orvyn, see if he saw anybody heading in this direction,' said Abigail decisively.

Several hours had passed and they still hadn't found Orvyn. Abigail confessed that they never normally spent Sundays together, so she didn't know what he got up to. They tried the church, watching the congregation as they left the service, no naked Saxon among them. They took a stroll down the high street, past Orvyn's pelican crossing, nothing. Des and Abigail were just following the footpath that marked the boundary of Orsworth when Des saw three figures up ahead, walking away from them. Two women, arms linked, and a cheerful old spaniel trotting along in front of them.

Des ran to catch up with them, his ball bag bouncing off his thighs, much like a talented hacky sack player showing off a new freestyle skill. Des realised this was the first time he had run in nearly twenty years. He felt as fit as a fiddle. Albeit, an eighty-four-year-old fiddle with massive knackers and a recent membership to the afterlife.

He caught up with Jarvis, Henrietta and Lucy before remembering he had no physical way of communicating with them. He knelt down next to the ditch, where Jarvis was sniffing. He held out his hand. Jarvis sniffed the stinging nettle right by Des' index finger. Jarvis' tongue lolled out of his mouth as if grinning a goofy smile, he continued to sniff the air and then cocked his leg and promptly urinated on the foliage. As Desmond watched Jarvis' steady stream he felt a sudden sting of sadness, Jarvis was no longer his dog. Henrietta gave a whistle and proffered a treat, half a cocktail sausage. Jarvis shuffled off after her, his tail wagging excitedly. It was a bizarre experience for Des, watching his old companion be happy with someone else, it was almost like seeing a loved one commit adultery right in front of your very eyes.

He stood and watched the three new friends make their way around the field. Abigail had just caught up, putting on a brisk walk so as not to embarrass herself by running. In her day a lady did not run, for the sports bra had not yet been invented.

'Good heavens, you're fast!' panted Abigail.

If there was one thing that could dig Des out of his slight slump, it was the opportunity for an innuendo and by thunder he took it. 'That's what my wife used to say,' said Des, with a wry smile.

They strolled the field, following the footpath, which was now leading them round the back of a horse filled paddock, which itself backed on to a newly converted farmhouse. The two of them were just discussing their favourite pastimes, Des' being cryptic crosswords and solitaire. Abigail was midway through explaining the rules of a game called "Hot Cockles" when they both saw a rather peculiar sight. An armless, naked man skipping gleefully around the paddock, taunting the horses with his spare arm and then throwing it as if expecting them to fetch it.

'Orvyn! What on earth are you doing?' Abigail screeched, much like a teacher who'd just caught many misbehaving miscreants.

'Abi! Desmondo! Wanna get in on the action? They're great this lot!'

Abigail politely declined on behalf of them both. She repeated, 'What on earth are you doing? Why are you harassing these nags?'

'Nags? These are not nags! These are Suffolk Punches, proper horses. Noble steeds, look at that one, look at that flank. Phwoar, what I wouldn't give to ride you.' Des saw the double entendre present itself but decided that now was not the time for wordplay.

'Orvyn, do please focus. Why are you here, in this field?' Abigail probed yet again.

The Saxon then went on to explain that he often frequented the field. This was his Sunday routine, he watched the lady of the house, a small blonde woman in a Barbour jacket, clean out the stables, then he'd wait for her to be gone before playing with the horses. Although the horses could not see Orvyn, they could sense his presence. If you ever see a horse get "spooked" and run around, it could simply be because a naked ghost is trying to coerce it into a game of blind man's buff.

There came the sound of a door opening, a beagle barking and a newly married middle-class couple arguing about whether or not the AGA had enough space to cook Christmas dinner or if they'd need to use the electric oven also.

'Really, darling, I think it'll be fine. I have prepared a roast before you know,' the lady of the house retorted.

'Yeah, yeah, I know, it's just that Mummy is very particular about what temperature her sprouts are cooked at, you understand?' responded the mollycoddled man.

'Peter, please, you're thirty-six-year-old, stop referring to your mother as "Mummy", unless you never, ever want to have sex again.'

'Sorry, Mads, I just want this year to be perfect. Christmas has already got off to an eerie start with that old boy topping himself in the woods.'

'Peter! Keep your voice down.'

At this, the naked eavesdroppers approached the house. They could go no further than the fence, which marked the village boundary. The house itself was technically in the neighbouring village of Lollingworth, but the field remained, as it always had, in Orsworth.

So here were Peter and "Mads", short for Madeleine, Des supposed, but he wouldn't be surprised if he was wrong. He'd read an article on the web last week about a man called Chris, whose full name had turned out to be Chrisophelus, so Des was prepared for all sorts of surprises. Peter was a bespectacled man with brown floppy hair of which even a 1999 Hugh Grant would be proud. He was an intelligent man, always looking to please anyone and everyone, particularly his mother. Peter is a typical Virgo.

'What makes you think he topped himself? Have they found something?' Mads asked as she put on her Le Chameau Wellington boots.

'Well, I picked up some pretty key evidence from the scene first thing this morning, dropped it off at the lab, Chief Constable Wendy Mack was there to meet me. She seems like a good egg, keen to get to the root of this case. Anyway, on the drive back, I got a call from the lab, saying that they found some fibres on the rock, fibres belonging to a pair of "Racing Green Joules Bamburgh gloves", the same gloves the old boy was wearing. So, Mack reckons that one of two things happened; he went off to the woods, picked up the rock and clonked himself round the head with it or, more likely, he fell, smacked his head, reached out to feel what he'd hit his head on and then died shortly after. Mack said our work is done now, she'll just deal with the formalities and admin of an accidental death in a public place.'

'Oh, that poor man. Oh, bless him... I'm sure if I did the sprouts in the AGA your mother wouldn't be able to tell any difference.'

The two carried on their previous conversation as they climbed the stile, the beagle leaping gracefully through the gap betwixt the panels and headed off on their Sunday walk.

Stillness.

The three ghosts didn't speak as the voices of Peter and Mads floated away on the wind.

'Who is that man?' asked Abigail, breaking the silence.

'No idea,' said Des.

'I saw him earlier, as it goes,' Orvyn piped in.

The other two looked at him as Orvyn told the gang that he'd seen Peter drive over his place of rest that very morning. When asked what else Orvyn remembered, he spoke of some words being imprinted on the side of the man's vehicle. However, when it came to recalling those words, they hit a bit of a hurdle.

It took Des and Abigail nearly half an hour to piece together "Forensic Services" from the fragmented information given to them by Orvyn, because Orvyn, despite Abigail's resistance, insisted on getting them to guess the words through a Saxonic version of charades.

They got "services" early on through Orvyn's demonstration of a tennis serve, his severed arm proving a useful racquet substitute. Of course, this then led them down one heck of a rabbit hole until Orvyn held up four heavily scarred fingers, did a pitiful impression of a songbird and then proceeded to pretend to vomit despite Des already shouting "forensic" after the second syllable had been guessed.

So, this Peter worked in forensics, did he? He was the one who was creeping around in the early hours, was he? Why on earth did he think it appropriate to talk so openly in public about such a sensitive topic? Des pondered this for a while, before embarking in an internal debate.

Lillian had worked as a nurse in A&E departments when she was younger, she used to bring back all sorts of stories and share them freely. But that was when we were alone together, reasoned Desmond. Then again, as far as this Peter fellow was aware, he and his wife were alone. They weren't to know that three undead spirits were privy to their conversation, one of them being the "old boy" they were discussing. This was a fair point. Des ended the debate.

The ghostly group began trundling along the footpath again. They discussed the recent developments surrounding the glove fibres on the rock. Des' insisted that he never touched the rock, but then again, he was in the process of dying, so admitted he might not remember accurately. It was now clear that Abigail had been correct in her earlier assumption that the local authorities would brush this one under the rug, an "accidental death", eh? Sod that. Nothing accidental about it. Desmond had been murdered, and it was now up to this eclectic trio to find out the perpetrator of such a heinous crime.

After discussing the case of Desmond's death for nearly two hours, they spent the rest of the day having their own debate about how best to cook brussels sprouts, which got so outrageously heated it culminated in Orvyn throwing his detached limb over the village boundary in a rage of fury and while he scampered off to the other side of the village to search for his arm, Abigail and Des headed back to Warren's Walk for yet another night of eternal rest.

Chapter Seven
Monday 15 December

*We sincerely apologise for Saturday evening's mistake in the typography it should have read, 'The body of Desmond Featherby, resident of Honeycomb Cottage, Queensbury Close was found this morning by a couple of **joggers**.' We do hope that no one was upset by this error and that you understand that we were merely trying to process this news and print it as quickly as we could. Many apologies from all at the Orsworth Gazette.*

Only one other person knew that Desmond kept the spare key to Honeycomb Cottage under his Agapanthus, Verity. She had been trusted with the knowledge when Lillian had fallen ill, so as to be able to pop in if assistance was needed. Verity was a good fifteen years Desmond and Lillian's junior, and she kept them young. Simon had been closer to their age, they made a rather spritely foursome in their prime, always having game nights, being the fittest amongst them Verity would always win, anything from tiddlywinks to tenpin bowling. Verity and Lillian had always been close, ever since they had moved to the village. They were a lovely little double act, reminiscent of Christine Baranski and Julie Walters in *Mamma Mia,* to give you a visual image.

The spare key however, was no longer under the plant pot by the back door. It was now sitting on the sideboard in Verity's front room. She had gone to pick it up shortly after Lucy and Henrietta had told her of Desmond's passing, they'd stopped by on their way back home with Jarvis, the last thing she wanted was some of the local youths finding it and raiding the place.

Desmond Featherby had not left a will; with no immediate family he saw little to no point in detailing who should inherit any of his possessions. The result of this uncharacteristic lack of organisation was that Honeycomb Cottage and all that dwelt within became bona vacantia. By law, Des' property was now in the possession of the Crown, but due to the laxed communication between local police force, government and the state, the dealings of the Featherby property were far from being dealt with.

This meant that at this current moment in time, nobody was keeping an eye on Des' house.

Meaning that nobody saw the shadowy figure, cloaked in disguise, masked against the night sky, shielded in darkness – in short, they were wearing black. No-one saw them slide the key in the door of Honeycomb Cottage and none saw them leave with a pilfered package hidden amongst their robes of obscurity.

Chapter Eight
Tuesday 16 December

I know we didn't follow the ghost's footsteps yesterday and as it happens; we won't do today either, the brutal truth is, being undead in a quaint Suffolk village doesn't leave you with an awful lot to do. So, while we're exploring other village residents, let's imagine that our gang of ghouls are killing time sharing tales from their past lives. Orvyn is teaching Desmond ancient Saxonic songs, Abigail is entertaining the other two by doing a one woman bear baiting show, all in mime. Des, in turn, tells the others the following story of how he and Lillian had met.

It was mid July 1958; Des had broken his nose playing for his village cricket team on Sunday afternoon. He'd gone out to the middle, batting out of his depth at number four, Copfield needed 31 runs off the last eight overs. An incredibly manageable score. The opposition, Hicklesbury, had brought on their youngster, only seventeen years of age but bowled a fast, in swinging ball, back of a length. Des had swung and missed twice. On the third, however, he hit the ball, or rather, the ball hit him, right on the bridge of his nose. He fell on to his stumps, giving away his wicket and blood streamed out of both nostrils all down his shirt, staining his whites.

A frozen bag of peas and two generously donated tampons later, he was sat in an A&E waiting room, looking like a bloodied walrus advertising a slowly defrosting bag of petit pois. A young nurse called his name, and he followed her as best he could, his view being obscured by Birds Eye's best and two swollen black eyes. She sat him down, filled out some paperwork and then, just as Des had built up the courage to ask her what time she finished, she cracked his nose back into place. Des hadn't experienced pain like that since he was in lower sixth when some of the bigger boys had tricked him into thinking that *Vicks VapoRub* was a suitable lubricant.

Just as the young nurse, Lillian Baldwich, was wiping away the blood from Desmond's chin, she agreed to a drink on Tuesday evening, seven p.m. at the Thatcher's Arms.

The rest, as they say, is history.

What am I like? I said we wouldn't be focussing on the ghosts in this chapter and here we are both getting distracted.

*

Annie Thorne, the daughter of Verity and Simon Thorne, was having a horrible stress dream.

She was racing down a poorly lit alleyway, which then turned into a beach. She struggled to run on the sand, feeling it swallowing her feet. Looking down, she saw the sand had turned into a thick, earthy sludge and was now absorbing her shins and her knees. She held her breath as she was dragged under the ground. Now in total darkness, she carried on trying to run. She drove herself forward, through what appeared to be branches and leaves, finding herself in a forest, she continued sprinting, this time she felt the presence of someone behind her, she could hear another set of footsteps crashing through the fallen foliage, snapping twigs with ease. She ran as fast as she could. Just as she turned to look behind, attempting to catch a glimpse of who was following her, the ground vanished. Now she was falling, falling towards a thick bowl of batter, she hit the surface of the mixture and could taste the grated carrot, she looked up. Her pursuer was leering over the side of the bowl, a hood covering their features, a silicon spatula in their gloved hand, they began to stir. The figure let out a harsh bark of laughter and as they did, hundreds of dime bags cascaded out of their mouth and into the bowl, then a massive hand forced itself into the batter, leaving fibres in its path. It scooped out a handful, with Annie sat on top, like a decorative figurine and just as she was being brought nearer the horrid, empty abyss of the mouth suddenly the teeth clamped down, barring her from entering. The teeth then began to chatter, making a hideous, deep rattling sound that ached Annie's ears. Annie began to panic, she could hear the voice, from behind the white wall calling out her name, 'Annie, Annie, I'm coming, Annie!'

'Annie, darling, I'm coming in.' Verity opened the door and popped a cup of tea on Annie's bedside table. She gently shook Annie, who started, blinking up at her mum, the sweat had dripped down her forehead into her eyes, sticking her fringe to her face on its way.

'Mum! I mean, morning, Mum, sorry' – Annie was breathing quickly – 'I was having a rather bizarre nightmare.' She took one big deep breath and picked up the tea her mum had brought her. 'I won't bore you with it, nobody ever finds other people's dreams as interesting as they do.'

Verity agreed and left the room. Annie had moved back in with her mum when Simon had become ill and she never left, she was hoping to move out in the near future once she was certain her mum was happy and also, more crucially, that she herself was financially secure. Annie sipped at her tea as she began to replay flashes of the nightmare she'd just had. She could still taste the carrot cake batter despite swilling her Typhoo around her mouth. The part of the dream that had shaken her most was the chaser, not Paul Sinha or Mark Labbett, who were both chasers in their own right, no, no, this chaser was no master quizzer but instead someone who was hot on Annie's tail.

In an earlier chapter, we discussed how Annie's bakery had struggled upon opening, but now, business was booming. The recent success has been down to a risky move from Annie after an entrepreneurial offer had come in from a visitor to the village. The visitor, one Malcolm Gibbs, had seen the suffering bakery and decided to pay

Annie a visit. One key piece of information I should add here is that for the last five years Malcolm has been one of East Anglia's most affluent drug dealers. Having the fortune of being best friends with anyone from barristers to bishops, he was rather untouchable. When Wendy Mack became Chief Constable of Orsworth, she made a statement ensuring that the drug culture spreading down from Norfolk would not seep into Orsworth, she had promised the locals that she would do her utmost to bring an end to the growing problem. However, she had dropped the ball. One weekend at the beginning of August, Wendy Mack was out of the village, attending a charity event in the capital, when who should sweep into the village like an infectious bacterium but Mr Malcolm Gibbs. Malcolm was a charming man, used to getting his way. He poked his head round the door of Annie's bakery, ordered a Bakewell tart, her first sale of the day and got straight down to brass tacks. He spoke of the potential for the bakery and gave Annie a proposition. He floated the suggestion of using the bakery as a place for his goods to be exchanged. Annie, of course, found this idea abhorrent, at first. But once Malcolm had sweetened the deal by assuring her that she needn't worry about getting into trouble, it wouldn't cost her a penny. In fact, he would give her a small slice for her troubles plus he assured her that all it would bring in a flurry of trade. His clients would buy her produce, with the goods encased within the cakes, pies and pastries. They would pay him for the drugs separately, so she needn't stress about handling large sums of money.

Annie said she'd have to think about it, she had asked Malcolm why he needed to change up his delivery system and he had been honest and said that his current base in Eyling, South Norfolk had burnt down after the thatched cottage next to it had caught fire due to the recent heatwave.

Needless to say, Annie agreed to this new venture. If she was ever going to move out of her mum's house, she needed money, and here was an opportunity to increase her income. Her business had indeed boomed, and she was now selling more cakes and bakes than ever before. Even people who weren't into narcotics were buying her normal produce just because they'd seen the busyness of the place. Malcolm had told his clients to wink three times at Annie as a subtle signal. This incredibly simple system worked remarkably well for over four months. Until a particularly busy afternoon shift a few days ago, when a familiar old man had entered the bakery, leaving his cocker spaniel tied to the lamppost outside.

Des had ordered his carrot cake but as he ordered it his contact lens in his left eye started to dry up.

Not wanting to cast aspersions, Annie had sold him the cocaine carrot cake. Whatever people got up to behind closed doors was none of her business and if an old boy in his 80s wanted to kick back, rack up a few lines of Columbian snow and enjoy a moist bake, then why shouldn't he. Nobody was going to get hurt, were they?

Chapter Nine
Wednesday 17 December

Four days ago, this village lost one of its oldest residents to a tragic accident. Desmond Featherby was found unconscious by two other locals in the early hours of Saturday morning. The area was taped off whilst we undertook standard investigations, the results show there was no foul play. Just an unfortunate incident. A mourning service will be held for Mr Featherby in the break between Christmas and New Year. Warren's Walk is once again accessible to the public, and I don't think this needs saying, but please tread carefully.

Official statement from Wendy Mack, local Chief Constable.

Published in the *Orsworth Gazette*, Wednesday, 17 December.

Wendy, arms behind her back, gave her statement outside the police station in front of a keen crowd. That's if you count: six people, three ghosts and a dog to be a crowd. Two reporters were present, one from the *Orsworth Gazette* and one from the *East Anglian Daily Times*. The latter left half way through after it was revealed that it was only an accident and not a potential murder story, he'd never be able to compete for print space with that, not against such huge regional stories like the lollipop ladies strike or the farmer who grew a spud that was the spitting image of Hugh Bonneville. The other attendees were of course: Verity and Annie, standing arm in arm; Lucy, Henrietta and Jarvis, who was giving his nether regions a good clean when the announcement was made; Des, Abigail and Orvyn made up the remaining crowd members.

After the statement was over, the crowd dissipated, and Wendy headed for her car, a Mazda2 Hybrid. She might not be able to stop an old man from slipping to his death, but she can certainly do her bit to reduce her carbon footprint. It was only a four-minute drive back to her house, some planet protectors may argue that she could lessen her emissions further by simply walking or cycling the distance, but Wendy Mack didn't give a damn what they thought.

She parked outside her front door, walked in, hung her pristine, navy blue coat up, popped her gloves on the sideboard and dropped her car keys into the bowl, where for so long the spare set of keys for their old house had lived, recently she had found a more suitable place for them. She strolled through to the kitchen and helped herself to a slice of Annie's finest. It was on the brink of being stale, perhaps only a day of life left in it. She was just finishing her rather dry mouthful when there came the sound of tyres on an inclined driveway. Looking out the window, she could see a white Range Rover Evoque parked alongside her Mazda2 Hybrid. She recognised that car, not just by the garishness of the model but also the personalised number plate, **M G1BB5**. Cue doorbell.

Chapter Ten
Thursday 18 December

The day following Mack's announcement, the ghosts walked in silence together, Des absentmindedly leading the group. It must've been the cocktail of emotions churning around his lifeless body that led Desmond to do the second most rebellious act of his life (or death), he led the group onto the out-of-season cricket wicket, despite it being clearly roped off. Des, to put it lightly, was out of control. He was off his fucking rocker. He tried to kick one of the poles that was supporting the rope, but his foot missed it entirely. A sad sight to see, dead or not. The momentum of his swinging leg brought him to the ground, where he sat for a split second before letting out a yelp, he had mistakenly put his entire body weight on his descended gonads. This did not improve his mood. His mind was rattling with all sorts of thoughts… *Who would actually come to his memorial? Has Jarvis understood what's happened? Will all of his possessions just be tossed in the bin?* One particular niggle rattled hardest: *Was he really going to spend the rest of eternity, gallivanting around this bloody village, in the nude, with two other sad, forgotten souls?*

'Bugger' was the only word he could conjure at that moment. Orvyn went over to console him, with his severed limb in his fully attached hand he patted him on the shoulder, so as to keep a safe distance should Des lash out.

'Tell you what always cheers me up,' Orvyn began.

'I am not in the mood to run around with ruddy horses or… or… or tickle sheep or play guess the body part,' muttered Des, failing to contain his frustration.

'No, no, none of those superb ideas. No, what never fails to cheer me up is sitting outside the bakery and playing "sniff it and say it", it's quite simple, you sniff what scent each baked good has and then—'

'You say it?' interjected Des dolefully.

'You played before? So, what do you reckon, you up for getting a whiff of brioche, or dare I say, a mince pie?' Orvyn was making himself giddy at the thought of smelling pastries. Seeing someone else cheerful used to irk Des when he himself was feeling low, however, he appreciated the effort made by the Saxon, so he agreed, penis clattering against his calves as he rose to his feet.

'Go on then, you lead the way.' Des half smiled.

Abigail was stunned, she, of course, had played a fair few games of "sniff it and say it", truth be told she thought it a rather silly game, but after spending centuries in the nether zone between life and rest, she accepted that not all past times were going to be thrilling. However, the prospect of distraction seemed to have raised Des' spirits, so why not have a game or two. She let the boys walk together in front, it made her rather happy to see them getting along so well. She thought, as many do, that one of the most heartwarming relationships is the friendship between two men, and she wanted to let it blossom. Also, she appreciated the view that they presented; they were both in surprisingly good shape, after all, and everyone needs to get their kicks somehow.

They turned onto the high street and saw the queue outside Annie's bakery. At least six people were lined up along the pavement. All of which were wearing slim fitting suits and tapping their feet impatiently, apart from the lad at the back, who was wearing a Thrasher hoodie, incredibly distressed baggy jeans and a pair of Vans, which were so scuffed and worn that the owner had resorted to using nearly an entire roll of duct tape in an attempt to preserve the shoes. The good news for the ghosts, mainly Orvyn, was that this meant there were lots of breads, buns and brownies to come. They had a long game ahead of them.

After playing the game for nearly three minutes, Des realised there was no real scoring system, as they couldn't physically taste the food, it was more-or-less a case of guess what flavours you smell and if the other two agree then you get a point. Orvyn had the unfortunate combination of being both extremely competitive and having a limited range of scent references, his goes all seemed to rotate between cabbages, onions or parsnips and anything that was covered in chocolate was most definitely mud and therefore smelt like mud, sweet mud at a push.

The Saxon got very excited when the lad, who had been at the back of the queue, came out with a carrot cake. The excitement seemed to brew from the delicately iced carrots atop the drizzled icing. The ghosts followed the young man round to a side alley so as to get a better look at the cake. Orvyn was jumping up and down, waving his detached limb above his head in celebration, shouting 'Thems orange parsnips, orange parsnips!'

'Carrots,' grunted Des.

'That's it, carrots!' carried on Orvyn, 'come on surely, surely that's a given! Point for Orvyn! Abigail you've got to agree surely tha—'

Orvyn stopped leaping up and down. They all stared in disbelief as the boy dug one of his fingerless gloved hands into the bake, wriggled it about, and then removed the sizeable dime bag he'd come for before throwing the cake in the rubbish bin. He pocketed it and began his journey out of the village. Orvyn was incandescent with rage. 'What is he doing? That manchild, what – he threw it away – I mean by all means eat it with your mitts but by heavens don't chuck it! The spoiled brat! I'll get him! I'll make him come back and eat the whole thing, orange parsnips and all!'

Des couldn't quite hear the rest of Orvyn's mutterings and curses as he was now chasing down the youth and shouting in his ears, as if the boy would hear him through the interdimensional planes of existence. Des was staring at the cake on the floor. Abigail was looking at him, her brow slightly furrowed.

'What was that little packet he retrieved from the cake?' she asked.

Des responded after a moment pondering, 'I'm not sure what it was exactly, but judging by its shape and size, I'd say it were an illegal substance of some kind. marijuana perhaps? That's what normally comes in those dime bags.'

'Oh right, is that like opium? I had a cousin who had an opium habit, odd chap he was, never blinked unless it was a full moon. Quite haunting really.' added Abigail.

'I suppose it's similar in some instances. I wouldn't know, I've never tried either of them. I only know about marijuana because my friend Brian used to smoke it. He said it helped settle his nerves. I just thought it stank.' Des briefly enjoyed the moment of reminiscing about Brian, he hadn't thought about Brian for a fair few days, whether that was because he'd forgotten about him or because the writer of this tale kept losing track of characters they'd introduced in earlier chapters it's hard to tell, but let's not get bogged down in who forgot who, I think it's a nice moment for Des to remember his friend before being brought back to earth by Abigail.

'But why was that man getting his drugs out of a cake? Surely there are far more simpler methods of delivery?'

'I don't know, I can't say I've ever found anything like that when I've gone to Anni—'

Des stopped himself mid-sentence. He had just remembered the carrot cake he had bought the day before he died. It was probably stale now, rock hard, something Des will never experience again. The cake was also likely to be mouldy, riddled with fungi, thankfully that's where the comparison between the two ends, Des had never had a STI in his life. Now I'm not suggesting that this carrot cake had a sexual infection, heavens no, but due to the natural processes of decay and given that Des' home was still being heated by his ever-faithful Worcester Bosch boiler, those processes would be well underway. Had that moist sponge been home to Class A drugs as well as a family of bacteria? Surely not, he would know. Wouldn't he?

Orvyn returned, panting and heaving. 'He's gone. Jumped into a sky-blue Citroen C4 Picasso and just like that' – Orvyn clicked his fingers – 'he shot off, no consideration for the Twenty's Plenty sign.' He let out a big breath before rallying himself. 'Right then, who's up for another game of sniff it and say it?

Chapter Eleven
Friday 19 December

Des awoke and was immediately filled with a sense of unease. I suppose sleeping where you were murdered would make most mornings pretty uneasy, but this one was particularly so due to the daunting task that lay ahead – getting into his house and checking the carrot cake for drugs. Now that might sound quite straightforward, but let's not forget this old, naked, deceased friend of ours can't actually touch, move or lift anything. So, what might be quite a simple task for you, or I is beginning to seem like an impossibility to Desmond.

The ghosts had decided yesterday that checking the cake for narcotics was a job that needed doing. When it came to discovering Des' killer, they had absolutely no leads whatsoever, but the discovery of an undercover drug trade being run through the village bakery proposed the idea that all is not as it seems in the quaint old village of Orsworth. If Des had been mis-sold an illegal substance, that possibly meant that someone else had been mis-sold a perfectly drug-free carrot cake and that someone might not have been too happy about it. Desmond didn't actually have a plan for gaining entry to his old home, he was hoping that on his walk to Honeycomb Cottage, a bit of divine inspiration would drop into his bald head.

Abigail and Orvyn waited for Des on the corner where the bridlepath met Queensbury Close.

'We thought we'd come and see what help we can offer.' Abigail smiled.

'Don't suppose you've somehow developed the ability to open doors since yesterday evening?' Des grunted back.

'Sadly not,' came the reply.

The trio headed for Des' old home. Des strode to the house and looked at his front step, there lay a heap of newspapers. The young girl had clearly not been informed that the resident at Honeycomb Cottage had died and would thus not be needing his morning and evening newspaper. There were eleven copies of the *Orsworth Gazette* in total, this morning's edition lay atop the pile and Des could just about make out the headline 'COD ABOVE!' He bent down to read the story.

Sylvia Brewer found several fish in her back garden yesterday evening and is claiming that they fell from the sky. She ensured the journalist she spoke to that she saw them dropping from up above, 'I was sitting there doing a bit of knitting, you know how it is, grandchildren are forever growing and I can only knit so fast ever since my arthritis worsened and then SLAP out of nowhere a fish falls down past the conservatory window and I jump up, look outside and there it is on the patio, stone dead, and while I'm standing there, SLAP SLAP PLOP, two more fish come falling from the sky, smacking the patio and a third lands straight in the watering can! It was most bizarre. Must be a message, mustn't it, from the big man in the sky, but I can't think what he's trying to tell me, perhaps it's to do with my great nephew becoming pescetarian. While this of course seems like a mystery, readers are reminded that Ms Brewer does live two doors down from notorious troublemaker Gwendolen Channon, who we all know, after last year's welly wanging competition, has got quite the throw on her.

Des shook his head, ridding it of the useless information he'd just taken on. He stared at his front door, willing it to open. Nothing happened. Three minutes passed with Des crossing his fingers, closing his eyes and wishing as hard as he could that his door would just suddenly spring open. Still nothing.

'Bugger.' Des breathed.

Delicately treading around his Buddleia, he tried to get a glimpse of the kitchen. He'd left the cake on the table, which he'd be able to see from the East facing window. Des had his fingers crossed, wishing that he'd develop X-ray vision in the next five seconds so as to be able to see if there were any narcotics in the cake.

He rested his head against the glass and framed his eyes with his hands to block out the winter sun's glare. He was looking at his kitchen. There was the mug tree that he had made Lilliar. for her 60th birthday with the Emma Bridgewater mugs cheerfully hanging from it. On the sideboard he could see their collection of cookbooks and in between Jane Grigson's *Vegetable Book* and Nigella Lawson's *How to be a Domestic Goddess* stood *Lillian's Recipes*, where Lillian had logged all of her favourite recipes throughout her life. She'd started that cookbook with her mum, shortly before her mother's passing. Des had barely given it a second glance in recent months, but now, looking through the window, it seemed as if it was his most treasured possession. He felt a wave of grief gush over his chest as he realised, he'd never see Lillian's handwriting again.

It took him a minute or two to remember what he was looking for, then he threw his eyes to the corner of the room where the round, oak table sat. Where the empty, round, oak table sat. The carrot cake wasn't there.

'That's odd,' said Des, coming away from the window, turning to face his naked friends.

'What's that?' returned Orvyn.

'The cake isn't on the table. I'm sure it was there when I set out with Jarvis, because I remember having to bat his nose away from it. How peculiar.'

'Peculiar indeed,' pondered Abigail. 'No-one else would've taken it or eaten it, would they?'

'Well, I'm the only one with keys, we used to keep a spare set under the Agapanthus round the back. But I can't see anyone breaking in just to have a slice of cake.' Des said blithely.

'It might not be just "cake" though, Des, heaven knows what else was in there. Did anyone else know your excellent hiding place for the spare set of keys?' Abigail sighed sarcastically.

'Only Verity as she used to pop round and help Lillian if I was out. But Verity wouldn't come round just to nick a carrot cake, would she?'

'You tell us, you knew her old boy,' said Orvyn.

'I thought I did,' responded Des despondently.

The three of them headed off for Verity's house, a seven-minute walk on a good day, but on this occasion, it took them over an hour as Orvyn wanted to play another round of "sniff it and say it". On three separate occasions during this next fixture, the ghosts saw a vehicle pull up, a passenger pop into the bakery and within two minutes be back in the car, cake in hand. All of these vehicles had been from outside the village. Orvyn didn't recognise any of the number plates, he was adamant about that.

They turned into Meadpath Street, coming towards them was a young mother and her younger son, the boy tripped over a loose paving slab. He grazed his knee, his mum picked him up, bouncing him in her arms, muttering to herself as she walked past the three ghosts, 'Bloody council, that's the third time this week.'

Abigail, Des and Orvyn discussed who was more at fault as they walked down to number 35, Verity's House. Des argued that it was the council, Abigail blamed the mother for not keeping an eye on her child and Orvyn thought the boy should look where he was going. They were still bickering as they arrived at number 35, but soon all stopped talking once they saw the scene before them. A man, a silver fox some might say, was coming out of the light pink door, its loose bronze knocker shaped like a soaring dragonfly rattling slightly in the gentle winter wind. He was halfway down the footpath when he turned and gave Verity, who was standing in the doorway, looking very satisfied, a wink. She smiled and closed the door. The man got into his abrasively large Range Rover Evoque, popped a Smint into his mouth and was just turning the engine on when Verity came hurrying down the path, Charles Tyrwhitt silk tie in hand, she threw it playfully through the passenger window before walking back inside, emphasising her hip movement as she strode. The man in the car smiled to himself before speeding off.

The three ghosts all stood there, rather bemused, as they watched the number plate **M G1BB5** turning the corner.

Chapter Twelve
Saturday 20 December

As a reader, if you've got this far, I'll assume you're just as curious as I am to find out who killed old Des. Well, we're not too far away from unmasking the killer, but before we get to that oh so crucial narrative juncture, we've got some gaps in the timeline to fill. Now, if you just take my hand and, with your spare hand, hold onto your hats, because we're about to find out what happened eight days previous when Annie sold Desmond Featherby a drug filled carrot cake.

Whilst we're filling in those gaps, let us imagine that our ghostly chums are spending this fine Saturday peering in through Verity's kitchen window, trying to get a glimpse of either the spare key to Honeycomb Cottage or the stolen, stale cake. To help pass the time Orvyn suggests what Verity and Malcolm might've been up to the previous afternoon and loudly guesses exactly what they were using the tie for. This makes Abigail blush and Des feel rather uncomfortable, especially when Orvyn proposes the image of Malcolm on all fours with Verity straddling him, using the tie as makeshift reins riding him around the sitting room shouting, 'Giddy up, Big Boy!' Oh, how the Saxonic mind works.

Now the very nature of Annie's secret side hustle, which is rather entwined with her professional, legal bakery business, makes it very difficult for her to deal with disgruntled customers. Which just so happened on Friday, 12 December. Several hours had passed since she had unquestionably given Desmond Featherby a cocaine filled carrot cake when a rather handsome man, late twenties, had set the bell tinkling as he'd entered the bakery. He wore a well fitted blue suit and his brogues were so well polished that they made the shiny countertop look as dirty as a communal yoga mat. He strolled up to Annie, winked three times and smiled. Annie smiled back. She knew the code; this must be another of Malcolm's "out of town" clients. However, she hadn't any special bakes left. The allotted stock had all been sold for the day, the last of which, a marijuana meringue pie, going to a very cheerful young lady who had said that Annie reminded her of a young Deborah Meaden. An odd compliment Annie had thought, but a compliment, nonetheless. The man coughed, winked yet another three times and began to look impatient.

'Excuse me,' he said, 'but when I place an order in advance, I expect it to be ready when I arrive.'

The man spoke with such brutish self-importance that Annie panicked and stuttered, 'Oh yes, sorry, of course, could you please possibly remind me what it is you ordered?'

The man spoke slowly as if he were speaking to someone unfamiliar with the English language, 'A treacle tart and,' now winking thrice for a third time, 'a carrot cake. If it's not too much trouble.' Patronising, belittling and condescending could all be used to describe how this blond man sounded. Annie got to work behind the counter, 'Ah, yes, I really am very sorry, um, here we are one treacle tart and one... carrot cake.'

The man sighed, snatched the baked goods from Annie's hands and stormed out of the bakery. The bell rang as he thrust the door open wide, he turned, looked at Annie and left it open, letting in the biting winter chill which Geoffrey Lloyd, the regional weatherman, had accurately foreseen. That man really doesn't miss. Realistically though, it was mid-December, it doesn't take a bachelor's degree to work out that it's going to be cold. Annie bustled over and slowly shut the door, she could see the man striding towards his sparklingly clean Audi A3, he was shaking his head.

The next hour was uninterrupted by customers, so Annie popped on Ronan Keating's innovatively named debut album, *Ronan* and had a sing-a-long whilst she began to shut up shop. She was just wiping down the table near the loos, Mr Keating's "Heal Me" soundtracking her as she went, when the bell went, signalling a new customer.

'I'm afraid we're closed,' she called behind her. No response. She turned around to repeat herself, 'Sorry, we're—' the word "closed" never quite made it to her soft palate. Malcolm Gibbs was standing in the doorway, smiling, but there was no joy behind those dreamy blue eyes of his.

'Hello, Annie.'

'Malcolm, hello.' Annie's voice seemed to be burrowing back down her throat, like a nervous mole who had just poked his head out of the ground only to see a tawny owl circling above his home and decided that his afternoon walk could wait. Whereas Malcolm's timbre was resonating powerfully from his rather broad and recently waxed chest.

'Annie, I've just had a call from a rather disgruntled friend of mine. He seems to have received... an "empty package" shall we say. No icing with his baked goods, if you catch my meaning. No cocaine in his cake would be, well, that would be the exact issue, in fact.'

'Ah.'

'Ah, indeed, Annie. Tell me, why did this particular customer not receive the correct order? You're not pocketing any of the produce yourself? Not stealing from me, are you?' Malcolm was probing Annie, not in the same way he probed her mother, this was more like an unwanted interrogation as opposed to consensual fornication.

'No, no, no. Of course not!' Annie spluttered.

'Good. Now, why the error?' Malcolm was looking down at Annie, his eyebrows slightly raised.

There would have been an uncomfortable silence here if it weren't for Ronan Keating's underrated track "Keep On Walking" keeping the tension at bay. Annie was nervous to respond, she had wondered that exact question during her cleaning. She had a theory but was cautious to voice it for fear of being wrong.

'Umm, well, I served everyone that winked three times, with the appropriate packages. So perhaps, I don't want to suggest anything, but mightn't there have been a miscommunication on... your... end?' Malcolm let this accusation hang in the air. Annie could feel her armpits beginning to sweat, her brow was already beading, and the back of her knees were more damp than the lightly scented moist towelettes you get at certain Indian restaurants. She wanted to turn the music off but was too afraid to move.

'You think I made a mistake?' he said coolly. Not cool as in a trendy hip hop way you understand, that would be bizarrely out of character. I mean cool as in icy or standoffish.

'I just—'

'I don't make mistakes, Annie. Now, there were five of my customers visiting you today, two this morning and three this afternoon, only four were served. I would like you to run me through those that you managed to serve properly.' Malcolm hadn't blinked in several minutes; Annie felt the glare penetrate her soul and she immediately started gabbling.

'Well, there was err, a blonde lady in a green dress first thing this morning, she had um, she had er, two ketamine coffee and walnut cakes. Then there was um, tall he's tall, comes in every weekday, he looks a bit like Martin Clunes, he had a cocaine croissant. In the afternoon there was, umm there was Desmond, the old man from round the cor—'

'Who?' Malcolms sharp voice cut through Annie's whimpering like a really excellent pair of scissors cutting through some cheap happy birthday wrapping paper.

'D… Des… Desmond, he's an old man, he's a friend of my mums.'

'And what did Desmond, friend of your mums have? Did he have a cocaine-filled carrot cake by any chance?'

'Yes. Yes, he did,' Annie said shamefully.

'And did you not think it rather odd for a man of that age to be getting gear from a local patisserie? Did that not throw up any red flags?'

'Well, yes, of course, but he did wink three times and it's not like I have a list of who is coming in day by day.' Annie fought back, bravely.

Malcolm's stoney face remained emotionless. Annie had messed up; she knew it and he knew it. The last thing Annie needed was for an old boy to overdose on high quality nose candy and for the police to come and do some sniffing of their own.

'What are we going to do?' asked Annie.

'What are *you* going to do?' replied Malcolm. 'This needs to be sorted out this evening. If you don't take care of this then I'll have to pay this "Desmond" a visit tomorrow.' And with that, he turned on his heel and strolled out of the door leaving it wide open.

Annie stood stock still, paralysed by fear and anxiety. "When You Say Nothing At All" was now accompanying her thoughts, it made her briefly think of Notting Hill... *What would Julia Roberts do if she were in my position?* pondered Annie. *Julia Roberts probably would never have allowed a regional drug dealer to operate through her bakery business in the first place. She was too good for Alec Baldwin in that film and she's too good for me,* she thought.

Fifteen minutes had passed since Malcolm's departure. Ronan Keating had stopped playing and Annie had locked up. She walked the long way home, her mind racing. How was she going to sort this? All she needed to do was get the carrot cake back from Desmond, but what if he had already cut into it, found the drugs and gone to the police? She'd be absolutely done for then. Perhaps he hadn't even had a slice yet, she could nip round in the morning and say there was something wrong with the batter, a piece of rogue eggshell perhaps, and offer him a fresh one? Could she wait until the morning? No. Malcolm had said this evening, or he'll sort it, what did that mean, what would he do? She had heard rumours of what he'd done up in Norfolk before expanding his business, the thought of Mr Featherby having his fingernails slowly peeled off made her spine shiver. She would have to get to Desmond before Malcolm. She checked her watch, 6:45 p.m., surely he'll be up. Taking a left down Merchant Street, she could see the signpost for Queensbury Close. Rounding the corner she saw the outline of Honeycomb Cottage; no lights were on in the house. The security light flicked on as she approached, she knocked gently. No answer, not even a bark from Jarvis. They must both be sound asleep already. Annie stood, not knowing what to do for all of eight minutes. She hurried home, deciding on the way that she'll head over first thing in the morning, if she was there early enough, she was sure she'd catch Desmond before Malcolm, and everything would be fine.

As Annie was walking down her road, she was tripped up by a loose paving slab. While she was picking herself up, brushing herself down and cursing the council for not fixing the pavement, who should walk past the far end of the road, dimly lit by street lamps and unnoticed by Annie, but an elderly man and his trusty cocker spaniel, enjoying the last few minutes of their evening stroll.

Chapter Thirteen
Sunday 21 December

Yesterday's sleuthing efforts hadn't been completely wasted, the three friends finally managed to catch a glimpse of Des' spare keys, noticeable by the faded Dunlop keyring. For context, Des had once bought a pair of Dunlop squash shoes and with them came a free keyring, an odd marketing ploy from an already successful sports brand, but here we are. I can sense that you're curious to know how good a player Des was, well his squash career was short-lived due to both his debilitating tennis elbow and also, crucially, the distinct lack of squash courts in the local area.

Our team of amateur detectives had all agreed that, after sighting the spare keys in Verity's house, she must have taken the cake, but since they couldn't see any sign of it, she must've disposed of it once she'd noticed the mould. That particular avenue of clues had come to a dead end. The friends didn't know where to turn and so while they waited for a new spark of inspiration, Abigail and Orvyn went to go and see the horses in the paddock, and Des went to go and visit Lillian.

Today marked Des and Lillian's 52nd wedding anniversary, or at least it would've done if either of them, ideally both of them, were still alive. Nevertheless, the memory of that snowy winter day is not forgotten. Sitting upon the tree stump by his wife's grave was Desmond Featherby, rearranging his knackers so as to stop his scrotum from pinching. He could almost hear Lillian's voice telling him off, 'Stop fiddling with yourself, we're at church, show some respect.' Des smiled at the thought of Lillian's gentle, dulcet tones. The Sunday service had just begun, the organist was playing "For Those We Love Within the Veil", which just so happened to be a favourite of Lillians. Des leant against the stump, closed his eyes, and replayed the best day of his life.

Des was standing at the altar, nervously tapping his feet. Lillian was late, obviously, why wouldn't she be? She was always slightly behind schedule every other day of the year. Why should this one be any different? Des turned around to look at the friends and family that had come all the way to Lower Portsleigh. It was a small affair, only their nearest and dearest, about twenty-five in total, it was a small congregation and yet St. Priam's Church looked close to bursting, all available pews were full. Des glanced to his left, where his best man, Rupert, his oldest friend from school, stood. Rupert was a tall, freckly young man with neat auburn hair, delicately combed to the side, giving him the appearance of a much more intelligent being. Des dabbed at his balding head with his handkerchief. He checked his watch, Lillian was twenty minutes late to their wedding, Des smiled feebly at his in-laws. Lillian's mother pursed her lips and turned to mutter something into her sister's ear. Des swallowed as much saliva as he could conjure up, his mouth had never been so dry, all the fluid in his body was evacuating through the soles of his feet and down the small of his back.

The organ sprung into life. Des looked around, there she was, Lillian, wearing the most incredibly white dress, her father, Derek, beaming on her arm. They walked down the aisle, ever so slightly out of time to the wedding march, Lillian stumbled as she neared Des, he caught her before she did any real damage to herself or the dress. Derek shook Des' hand and winked.

'Sorry, I'm late' – Lillian smiled – 'forget my garter, didn't I!'

The vicar pretended not to hear this and ploughed on with the ceremony. It was all a blur to Des, he just stared at Lillian throughout the entire service, she'd never looked so perfectly angelic. He blinked and he was walking down the aisle, his now wife on his arm. He just couldn't stop smiling, even his mother-in-law managed to curl the corners of her lips as they walked past. That evening they danced, drank and frolicked in the snow. It was a short walk from the church to Lillian's parents' house, where they were having the reception. Derek gave a wondrous speech, displaying his love for his daughter with one hand and gently ribbing Desmond with the other, sadly Rupert's speech was not so good. Rupert was an amateur magician; I use the word amateur generously. He had decided to use this opportunity in front of an audience to try out some of his latest tricks. Seventeen minutes of watching his best friend fumbling a deck of cards and attempting to retrieve a handkerchief from his mother in law's blouse was enough for Des. He signalled hastily to Rupert to finish up. Rupert gave an extravagant bow during which he accidentally hit his head on the top table, knocking himself unconscious. A smattering of uneasy applause filled the room, Derek rose to his feet and saved the day by making an excellent joke about a magician who lost his magic and was then henceforth known as Ian, before lifting Rupert over his shoulder and propping him up in his chair. Des' speech was short and heartfelt, not quite as memorable as Rupert's perhaps, but it had most certainly been well received. Des was not a public speaker. He'd stood up to deliver his toast and say his speech, but his palms were so sweaty that they'd soaked the paper on which his speech was written. The ink had run, making the words totally illegible and he had been incredibly flustered, so repeated the story of how they had met, always a safe bet and then raised his glass to his new wife and announced his undying love for her. It was incredibly sweet.

Roast beef followed the speeches, accompanied by what felt like buckets of red wine, which, combined with her dyspraxia, proved disastrous for Lillian's dress. After a quick outfit change, they had their first dance, Lillian in her dressing gown and Des in his morning suit, they looked quite the pair.

The evening came to a close and the two of them sloped up to Lillian's bedroom, her parents had kindly offered them the whole house for the evening, they'd be staying down the road with a friend. As the bedroom door closed, they looked into each other's eyes and grinned so wide the Cheshire cat would've been impressed and then slowly Lillian pushed Des onto the bed, slid off her dressing gown, climbed on top of him and out of absolutely nowhere, began urinating on him.

Wait, wait, wait – hang on, that's not quite what happened. Des, eyes still closed, shook his head trying to remember his wedding night. He went back into that memory, there he was, tie askew, lying back on the bed and there was Lillian, leg cocked, pissing all over him. Now really, that can't be right! Des came back to the present and opened his eyes.

'Ah,' he said, 'that makes a lot more sense.'

It was not his late wife but Jarvis, who was cheerfully finishing up a rather lengthy wee. Des stood up abruptly, looking at his torso he realised that he was free of urine but the tree stump that he'd been leaning against was now firmly marked as Jarvis' territory.

He shook his head again, trying to rid the now tarnished memory of his marriage consummation from his mind. Des followed Jarvis with his eyes, he was trotting along the icy footpath back to Henrietta, who then clipped his lead on to his collar. He seemed happy; his tail was wagging so fast it looked as though he might take off from the ground. Des' watched as Jarvis and Henrietta waited outside the front of the church, the service had just finished, and the congregation were coming out. Annie was hurrying, heading back to open up the bakery for the afternoon no doubt and Lucy was also in amongst their number. Jarvis, allowed a bit of distance by the new and expensive extendable lead in his new owner's hand, bounded up to Lucy and rolled onto his back at her feet, clearly suggesting that she rub his belly. She did so. The three of them walked off in the direction of home. Des smiled to himself, looked down at Lillian's headstone and whispered, 'At least he's happy, eh?' and with that he decided to head to the paddock, his penis swinging dolefully in time with his stride.

He found Abigail and Orvyn in the field which backed onto Peter and Mads' house. As he approached them, Abigail nudged a distracted Orvyn, who was busy trying to mount a horse, despite not being able to actually physically touch the animal.

'All right,' said Des, 'how's your morning been?'

'It's been this for hours, Orvyn is convinced he'll be able to ride a horse, he just needs to 'catch it off guard.' Abigail's eyes rolled in their sockets as she spoke but then she caught Des' eye, smiled and said, 'Happy anniversary, Desmond.'

'Thank ye, Abigail. One of the odder anniversaries I will say. Don't suppose you've seen or heard anything that'll help us in our investigation? That Peter bloke hasn't popped his head out the door and given us any more information by any chance?' inquired Des.

'I'm afraid not. However, on our walk over here we did see that white car again, the one we saw leaving

Verity's house. This time, we saw it arriving. We saw the same man get out and head inside. He was only in there for about fifteen minutes, clearly whatever he was doing didn't take very long.' Abigail informed him innocently.

'I'll bet it didn't,' scoffed Des, 'come to think of it, I didn't see Verity coming out of the church this morning. I wonder why she's sneaking this man in and out of the house. Maybe she doesn't want Annie to find out.'

'Or maybe *he* doesn't want Annie to find out?' bounced back Abigail.

Chapter Fourteen
Monday 22 December

There was an almighty rumble as the Kingsmill truck, shortly followed by the Hovis van, came rattling into Orsworth. It was as if they were having a competition to see who could deliver their produce to the local Budgens first, it was a close call, so close in fact that you might say it was... 50/50.

Orvyn was awoken by the commotion. He was a deep sleeper but even he could be roused by two hefty vehicles driving directly over his place of rest. He clambered to his feet, picked up his arm, gave it a stretch and wandered over to where the two delivery drivers were racing to drop off their respective loaves. Orvyn watched quite happily for a good four minutes. If he could have done, he would've put his money on the Hovis lady, whose system was proving much more efficient than Mr Kingsmill, who, to be quite frank, had a sloppy technique. Six minutes later, Orvyn watched as they both awkwardly negotiated a seven-point turn in the high street before speeding out of the village.

Orsworth was a peaceful village, especially at this time in the morning, before the streetlights filled the pavements with their artificial glow. Orvyn strolled the streets, guided by his memory more than anything. He came to Meadpath Street, the oldest street in the village. Orvyn had been around when it was known by its maiden Germanic name "*medustig*" the rough translation being "path to the mead hall". Over the years it has been anglicised and now it is simply Meadpath Street, which rather annoys certain local lexophiles as "path" and "street" have such similar meanings, it sounds needlessly repetitive. There was actually a petition brought forward in the 1940s to officially change it to Mead Path and get rid of the word "street" altogether but understandably the village decided to focus their attention on the Second World War rather than the name of a road.

Orvyn was drawn to the road, for it was the only place in the entire village that was slightly illuminated. Classically, people tend to use the old moth to a flame idiom whenever someone is attracted to something. You might have thought I was going to compare Orvyn's interest in the light to that of a moth. However, after a quick Google search it was made clear that moth season in the UK is May–October and if I had compared Orvyn to a moth, you may have thought that either it was a moth with very poor time management or, worse, you might have thought me ignorant and uninformed about the habitual routines of our winged friends. So, in order to avoid that confusion, I decided not to mention moths. At all.

The kitchen light at number 35 was on and there was movement inside. Orvyn, curious, wandered down the street, arm swinging by his side and looked into the kitchen, where he could see Verity pottering about. He could see by the clock that it was now 5.45 a.m., Abigail had taught him to read both analogue and digital clocks, having taught herself during the late twentieth century. He watched as Annie walked into the room and although the double-glazed nature of the window muffled their voices slightly, he could just about make out every word that was said...

'Play Jack Johnson, Alexa,' implored Verity exasperatedly, 'please play.' She had evidently been struggling with the Amazon Echo for a good few minutes.

'How Many Times, Mum' – Annie sighed – 'you have to say Alexa at the beginning, otherwise it won't work.'

'"How Many Times" by DJ Khaled on Amazon Music,' chimed in Alexa, perched on the windowsill.

'Oh, here we go.' Annie sighed.

Pour a cup for the bitches that ain't scared to get down—

'Alexa, be quiet.' Alexa obeyed. Annie asked the device to play Jack Johnson, and it obliged, filling the room with his third studio album, *In Between Dreams*. Annie popped the kettle on and readied her KeepCup for her morning coffee, which she'd use to keep her hands warm on the walk to the bakery and then drink it while she was opening up.

'What are you doing up at this time anyway, Mum?' she asked.

'I wanted to catch you before you left for work. There's um... something I want to talk to you about.' Verity seemed nervous, anxious to broach the subject.

Annie's mouth went a touch dry, naturally the worst case scenario flew to the forefront of her mind – her mother had found out that she was in cahoots with notorious drug dealer, Malcolm Gibbs and she was about to tell her how disappointed she was and despite the fact that she was her daughter, she'd have to report her to the police.

Annie peeled a banana with slightly trembling fingers before saying, in the most nonchalant manner she could manage, 'Okay, yeah, what is it, Mum?'

'Umm, well, it's just that I er, I want... I want to tell you that I've met someone,' Verity stuttered her way to a relatively confident statement.

Mistaking Annie's look of befuddlement for a look of disgust, she quickly reasoned, 'I know, I know this might be difficult for you, but I get lonely and ever since your father passed away, I've just got this big gaping hole and it needs filling.'

An unfortunately long silence hung in the air after this sentence, broken only by the boiling kettle. Annie slowly placed down her banana, she didn't feel much like eating anything now, let alone a phallic shaped fruit. She picked up the kettle and poured the water over her Douwe Egberts Pure Gold instant coffee, burning the grounds slightly.

'Who is he?' asked Annie, turning her back on her mother as she headed for the fridge to retrieve the milk.

'He's a lovely man, very handsome. Troubled past but he's... untroubled now, I really think you'd like him if you got to know him, he's called Malcolm.' beamed Verity like a giddy schoolgirl confessing a crush to her best friend.

Annie froze as she opened the milk, she had a slight lump in her throat. Surely not. 'Malcolm?' she said, trying to sound blasé, ignoring the swelling in her gullet.

'Yes, Malcolm. Malcolm Gibbs. Now, I'm aware you might've read about him, he used to be involved in some nasty business in Norfolk a few years back, but that's all behind him,' assured Verity, 'he's moved on from that life now. He told me. He told me it's all over; he now co-owns a Garden Centre with his brother, just off the A140 near Bawesbury.'

Annie could feel her mother's eyes on her. She tried to act normally, but failed almost instantly when she went to give the milk bottle a shake, forgetting she'd already taken the lid off. Milk everywhere. The surface top was drenched, her banana doused in semi-skimmed but luckily a fair amount landed in her Keep-Cup, so not all bad, eh?

As she wiped down the surface with several squares of kitchen roll, muttering to herself that, 'One sheet was almost definitely not "Plenty".' She turned to her mum, unable to withhold her incredulity. 'You're sleeping with a drug baron? That man is East Anglia's Kingpin!'

'Oh please, Annabelle, this isn't an episode of Miami Vice. I've told you he's through with all of that, he gave it all up when he opened up the garden centre.'

'A bloody garden centre! Oh yeah, much more lucrative, I'm sure. Swapped in the poppers for poppies, has he? How long has this been going on then?'

'Only a week or so. Not long, please don't get upset. I just wanted to tell you before you heard some other way or by walking in on us—'

'Yes okay. Thank you.'

Another bout of silence filled the room. Jack Johnson was doing his best to lift the mood.

'Hang on, wait a minute, how did you even meet?' asked Annie.

'Well, it was the morning that poor old Desmond passed away. I was just walking back from Queensbury Close, I'd gone to grab Des' spare keys, to keep them safe and we met on our road, just near that loose paving slab. I remember, I was still in shock from hearing about Desmond, I tripped, and he caught me. He got me upright and asked if I was okay, he brushed my hair behind my ear, I felt the softness of his gloves brush my cheek. I'd recognise that sensation anywhere Joules Bamburgh gloves, the same gloves that your father had. I held his hand, and he gave mine a comforting squeeze before seeing that I made it safely inside. He popped round the next day just to check on me and well, we've seen each other nearly every day since, it's really been a whirlwind romance, passionate, physical—'

'Right!' interjected Annie, 'okay, great.'

She was nodding fervently like one of those Churchill insurance bobblehead bulldogs that people have on the dashboards of their Ford Fiestas. She didn't know what to say, her mother was sleeping with the man who had threatened to "pay a visit" to Desmond Featherby to protect his drug dealing business and then the next morning Desmond had been found dead. As far as Annie was concerned, her mother was dating a murderer and a mad man not to mention a criminal overlord. Why was Malcolm interested in her mum though? I mean she kept herself in shape there's no doubt about that, she looks great for her age, but to strike up a relationship the day after he'd intimidated Annie. It all seemed a bit manipulative. *Unless,* thought Annie, still nodding away, *he's only sleeping with her to punish me for making that mistake.* Now that does seem like the kind of thing a sociopathic drug baron would do.

'I've got to go to work, Mum, I'll see you later.' Annie threw the damp, milk-sodden paper still clutched in her hands, into the bin, grabbed her coffee and then walked out of the front door, straight past a naked Orvyn who was trying to commit to memory everything he'd just heard.

*

It was still dark when Des opened his eyes, he propped himself up on his elbows and looked from his place of rest to the village. The streetlights flicked on; a low humming could be heard from one of the many faulty bulbs. Desmond got to his feet and walked over to where Abigail lay, she too had just awoken.

'Morning, Desmond, to what do I owe the pleasure of this early greeting?' She yawned.

The two of them were just exchanging pleasantries when they heard a wheezing pant coming from the path leading to the village. It was Orvyn, scampering over, severed arm waving in the air.

'And good morning to you, Orvyn, why might I ask, are you charging about so early in the morning, Christmas Day isn't for another three days you know?' teased Abigail.

'Shhh! Please don't speak Abi, sorry, it's just I need to tell you what I've just heard and if you speak then I might forget and if I forget then I won't remember!' cried Orvyn.

It took Orvyn a surprisingly long time to recall what was a relatively short conversation but that might be because he went off on a tangent about whether fridges were really the best place to keep milk seeing as milk came from cows and goats and as far as he was aware cows and goats didn't live in fridges, they lived in fields, so why didn't people keep their milk in fields?

Once Orvyn had finished recounting his story there was a moment of quiet.

'So, let me get this straight,' said Abigail, 'Annie's mother is being courted by this Malcolm, who is the man we've been seeing, and he is also the man who is running this drug business through Annie's bakery?'

'Unless there is another drug baron kicking about these parts, then yes!' exclaimed Orvyn.

'Crikey, what do you make of all of this, Des?' asked Abigail. 'Des?'

Des was standing completely still.

'Des?' Abigail repeated.

'Desmondo?' said Orvyn, waving his bodiless arm in front of his face. 'You okay?'

'Gloves' – Des breathed – 'Bamburgh gloves.'

'What about them? That's what that Malcolm fellow was wearing when he… when he—' it only now hit Orvyn when he was saying it aloud for the second time.

'He was wearing Bamburgh gloves. The morning I died… according to that Peter, the fibres found on the rock belonged to a pair of Joules Bamburgh gloves… bugger.'

'Well, I'll be damned, here I was thinking I was providing the group with some juicy gossip when actually I've gone and solved the case!' cheered the Saxon.

'Yes. Well done, Orvyn, but perhaps now isn't the time for celebrating.' Abigail patted his attached arm; she could see that Des was still reeling from this revelation.

'Ah yes. Sorry, Desmondo mate,' grunted Orvyn.

Des couldn't believe it. He had been killed by the most notorious drug baron that rural East Anglia has seen for the last 250 years. All because of a slightly dry contact lens.

Chapter Fifteen
Tuesday 23 December

Snow was falling, the flakes lightly covering everything from headstones to letterboxes. The path leading to the church doors had been cleared in preparation for the evening carol service. Reverend Daniels stood by the door, welcoming in the congregation, a Fox's Glacier Mint doing the best it could to mask the smell of Benson and Hedges on her breath.

Abigail, Orvyn and Desmond had spent the rest of the previous day and the majority of today planning how on earth they were going to communicate to the living folk that Malcolm Gibbs had murdered Des. They hadn't got very far, but they had all agreed that if they were to be able to contact anyone then the vicar would surely be their best bet. Since he and Lillian had moved to Orsworth in the mid-1980s, Des hadn't missed a carol service and seeing as they were aiming to transmit some sort of message to Reverend Daniels, the ghosts had all agreed to attend the carol service, observing from outside the stained glass window which depicted Judas' betrayal. They'll then approach the vicar after the service, when surely her connection to the spirit world would be at its strongest, if such a connection existed.

Our ghoulish gang stood opposite the vicar watching the attendees enter the church, everyone was making an appearance, even the minor characters who we've only heard mentioned briefly. Verity and Annie were there, Verity evidently taking a break from her passionate lovemaking, Peter and Mads also passed through the threshold, the brussels sprout debate seemed to have been settled but now they were bickering about sleeping arrangements.

'You know Mummy needs a firm mattress for her osteoarthritis, perhaps we could—'

'If you even think of suggesting sharing a bed with your mother Peter, I swear to all that is holy, I will leave you,' Mads hissed.

Peter recoiled as he mumbled, 'Sorry, Maddonabella.'

As they strode past them, Abigail and Des caught each other's eye, raised their eyebrows, and shared a "I wouldn't want to be pulling a Christmas cracker with Maddonabella any time soon" sort of look.

Henrietta and Lucy came next, nervously nattering about whether Jarvis will be okay on his own for the next hour or so, this made Des smile, knowing that his old friend was being well looked after. Jarvis' new owners were swiftly followed by Chief Constable Wendy Mack, hands in pockets, striding confidently, nodding curtly to Reverend Daniels as she briskly wished her a merry yuletide. Beatrice Allen, the head of The Neighbourhood Watch and Women's Institute shook the vicar's hand as she passed before being accosted by Gwendolene Channon who was waiting for her inside, trying to claw her way back into the WI no doubt. Well, sorry Gwen, you can't commit arson and identity fraud on the same day and be surprised when there are consequences. PC Dunston and PC Bates, remember them? Well, they were there too, they absolutely love a Christmas song, Bates' favourite is O Holy Night, which, to be fair to them, is an absolute corker of a carol. Dunston's favourite is In the Bleak Midwinter, not the most cheerful but it certainly warms those festive cockles. Finally, the young mother and son the ghosts had seen on Meadpath Street last Friday trudged in, also with them was the young girl who was continuing to deliver Des' newspaper, despite his death. All of these characters took their seats and Reverend Daniels followed them inside.

The ghosts peered in through the aforementioned stained-glass window, the church was full to the brim. They could make out all of the characters we've just mentioned, the rest of the congregation were blurred faces, background artists if you will, folk who have no impact on our narrative as they didn't buy any illegal baked goods nor did they have a personal connection to our protagonist, Desmond Featherby.

The organ started up and the gathering gave "Once in Royal David's City" their best effort, several brave souls ambitiously attempting the high note on "lowly", none of them quite hitting it. The hymn finished and the congregation took their seats. The carol services in

Orsworth were never particularly lengthy and everyone knew why, Reverend Daniels was keen for the party to move from the church to the Common Inn as quickly as possible. The order of service used to consist of a few carols, a reading from Beatrice and finally the service would come to an end with Reverend Daniels doing some form of sermon about being kind to one another and treating others with the same respect and love that you would hope to receive in turn. The usual stuff. It also used to be tradition for the Chief Constable to do a reading, however Wendy Mack had made it quite clear that she would not be standing at the pulpit anytime soon. This year was no different, the carols came and went, Beatrice did her reading with the exact same monotone, expressionless delivery as she had done for the past eight years and at last it was time for Reverend Daniels' moment in the spotlight.

'Is it nearly over, Desmondo? I can't stand to listen to their screeching anymore, sounds worse than when my uncle drowned that sack of cats,' groaned Orvyn, who had stopped looking through the window and was now sitting on the ground, picking away at the sinewy hole where his arm used to meet his shoulder.

'Nearly done, Orvyn, I just want to hear what the vicar has to say,' Des responded.

The vicar began by drawing parallels from today's society to that of Jesus' time before moving on to the importance of caring for those around us for whom Christmas can be a difficult and lonely period.

'And lastly, I would like you all to put your hands together and join me in a minute's silence, during which we will remember those members of our community who we have lost this year, Meredith Applecart, Jonathon Dillingsby, Sophie Hunt, Maurice Lollings and most recently of course, Desmond Featherby. Once the minute is up, I shall lead us all in the Lord's prayer. After which those who wish to, can join me in the Common Inn,' he added in an undertone.

In unison the congregation put their hands together and bowed their heads. Des looked at them, all these people, some who he had never spoken to before, taking a moment to remember his life. His eyes smiled as they flicked from pew to pew, it was really quite touching. Then his eyes settled on a pair of hands near the back of the church. His smile faltered. Malcolm Gibbs was not the only person keeping their hands warm with specifically branded knitwear. Somebody else was wearing a pair of Joules Bamburgh gloves, but what was more, this pair were racing green, the exact same colour Desmond once wore.

Chapter Sixteen
Wednesday 24 December
Christmas Eve

'Twas the night before Christmas, when all through the Vill,
Not a sound was being made, it was quite, quite still.
Annie's bakery was shut for two whole days,
Can't get any coke to sniff nor weed to blaze.
The ghosts were all sleeping, as nude as can be,
Their privates, like our murderer, quite, quite free.
This peaceful old village, once noble and great,
Was now the—

Oh, for heaven's sake, I'm not going to do the whole poem, do you know how ridiculous that would be? Such a drastic shift in writing style and structure at this stage of the tale would be a complete spanner in the works. I also wasn't sure about the word "Vill", but it is a word, it's a mediaeval unit of land and the origin of our word village. It's also a valid scrabble word, which is the main reason I felt comfortable enough to use it in the opening line of the above poem. It doesn't look like a word though, does it? Vill.

We're all still wondering who the ruddy hell killed Desmond Featherby, aren't we? We all thought Orvyn had cracked it when he revealed that Malcolm Gibbs wore Joules Bamburgh gloves, however the way that last chapter ended seemed to insinuate that there is another suspect amongst our local residents. Well, the easiest way for you and I to discover who felled Des is to rewind the clock, flick backwards through our A3 desk diary, scroll upwards in our Apple calendar, go back in time basically. Yes, that's right, the rest of this chapter will retell the events of Saturday 13 December, only this time round, we'll see it from the killer's perspective. Thankfully, this person, advised by their expensive therapist, keeps a personal journal and helpfully noted down the incident which occurred on Saturday morning and luckily you and I have been given permission to peruse this diary. Please prepare yourselves and get ready for some first-person narration.

I didn't sleep well last night. My mind was distracted after yesterday's conversation. Why, oh, why do we ever let other people get involved with our business? If there is one thing I've learnt over the last few years, it's, "If you want something done properly, do it yourself". So that's what I did. I popped my work things on, donned my hat and gloves before wrapping myself in my partner's old trench coat to complete the outfit. I was out the door at approximately 08:35. I knew where this Desmond character lived after having seen him and his wretched spaniel on several occasions. Turning the bend I could see them in the distance, just entering Warren's Walk. I quickened my pace. Very few people ventured near Warren's Walk as it is rumoured to be haunted, no such thing as ghosts, load of old pish if you ask me. I followed the old man and his dog, I hid behind a gnarled hornbeam just out of ear shot, watching as the latter chased after a squirrel. That was my opportune moment to strike. Picking up a nearby rock and grasping it in my gloved hands, I swiftly crept up behind the frail pensioner. Job done.

People might wonder if it was necessary to kill an innocent old man or if I felt any guilt or remorse? The truth is, when you're working in a business like mine, you need to be ruthless, you have to have the balls to pull the trigger because if you have any second thoughts or show any sign of weakness, you might find that next time round, the gun is aiming at you.

So, I killed him. One blow. That's all it took. I cracked his skull with one powerful stroke. Initially, I was going to take the rock and dispose of it in the river, but then I saw that Desmond and I were wearing the exact same gloves – a smart pair of Joules Bamburgh gloves. I had bought them for my partner years ago, but he refused to wear them, he said that real men didn't need gloves. I think his dry, chapped skin would strongly disagree. What an absolute tube.

It was the perfect setup. I left the rock. It would simply look like an accident, an old man fell, hit his head on a rock, reached out to grab it, which explained any fibres on the rock, and then died shortly after. This thought process took a mere twelve seconds, I darted out of the woods while that daft spaniel was still distracted and headed straight for work. It's only round the corner from Warren's Walk. I took my hat and gloves off as I went, the coat came off as I entered the building. After I had hung up the trench coat, I made a quick coffee and sat down at my desk.

There was still one problem that needed solving, how to get the cocaine-filled carrot cake out of Desmond Featherby's house?

There was a knock at my door, it was PC Bates. Apparently, there had been an incident in Warren's Walk, and they were going to go and check it out, I told them to take Dunston with them and said that I'll be there once I finished my coffee.

I've got it, I'll pop to the clinical lab once his body and belongings have been transferred. I need to meet the team over there anyhow, and now seems as good a time as any. While I'm over there, I'll take the spare keys for our old house and swap them with Des, shouldn't be too hard. I'll then help myself once it's dark. I tell you what Malcolm is lucky that I'm a boss who isn't afraid of getting their hands bloody, I'm expecting a substantial "thank you" for getting him out of this mess. I haven't had to get this involved since we moved our operation down from Norfolk.

There we are, who'd've thunk it, a corrupt copper. Bet you've never heard that one before.

Chapter Seventeen
Thursday 25 December
Christmas Day

It is true what they say... 'Where there's a ding, there's a dong.' Well, that's certainly the case when it comes to the tolling bells of Orsworth Church, which could be heard dinging and indeed, donging, in both the physical and astral planes of existence.

'Happy Yuletide blessings!' cried Orvyn as he scampered in the direction of Warren's Walk. The sun had barely begun to rise and yet the Saxon had been up for a while, tearing around the village spreading as much cheer as he could. Orvyn loved the festive period. Naturally, he refused to refer to today as Christmas Day as he was raised by pagans, who knew it to be "Yule". There were no stockings or presents in the afterlife and seeing as Orvyn couldn't physically get hold of a yule log to burn in commemoration of the holiday, he simply pretended to set fire to his severed arm. Ah tradition.

Des and Abigail heard the shouts and came to greet him where the footpath met the treeline.

'Season's greetings, Orvyn,' they said in unison.

The three friends were all surprisingly chipper, given that they'd spent the whole of yesterday discussing Desmond's murder. They had finally all agreed that Wendy Mack, the Chief Constable of Police was the killer. Of course, they had no idea of her true motive, but the gloves and specifically the colour of them was the crucial piece of the puzzle and they couldn't ignore it. They only managed to rule out Malcolm Gibbs as a suspect after loitering outside Verity's house for the entire afternoon, hoping he'd pay her a visit. Eventually he did. The white Range Rover with its personalised number plate screeched to a halt. The ghosts hid behind the garden fence of number 33, waiting until Malcolm had gone inside, before rushing over to his car and peering through the windows. There was, of course, no need for them to wait for Malcolm to enter the house. They were ghosts. Invisible ghosts. Invisible naked ghosts. But you already knew that. If you forgot that they were naked, then think of it as a friendly reminder that they have been naked this entire time, areolas and all. Des was the one who spotted Malcolm's gloves in the passenger footwell. They must've slid off the seat when Mr Gibbs slammed his brakes on only moments before. Indeed, they were Joules Bamburgh gloves, as Orvyn had reported, but the colour was no racing green, it was that of French navy blue.

The ghosts had cracked the case. However, they still had no way of contacting the real world, thus justice could not be wrought upon Wendy Mack. It was now a waiting game. 'The truth will out,' as William Shakespeare once said, which is all well and good, but he never said how long it would take.

Des was frustrated that he would never know why he had been killed. If anything, it was more annoying knowing who had done it and having no idea why than it was being completely clueless about the whole situation. The ghosts sat around Orvyn's arm, imagining that it was producing warm flames like the yule log it feigned to be, they were passing the time talking about their respective festive traditions. Abigail told the others how they used to feast and dance and feast and dance and feast and dance for twelve whole days.

'Didn't you get indigestion?' Des snorted, making himself laugh but nobody else.

The nattering continued. Abigail was not a boastful lady, nor was she oblivious to her privilege, however she couldn't help but name drop every now and then, 'One Christmas we were invited to Hampton Court Palace by James I, sadly Shakespeare had died a few years before so I never got to meet him, my brothers did though. I understand that he's as popular now as he was back in the day?' She looked at Des for a response that never came. 'Anyway, I still got to meet James and Anne, we watched Twelfth Night which everyone said was terribly good. It wasn't for me, if I'm honest. Too lovey dovey.'

She went on again about the extravagant feasts they had, the roast turkey, goose, the scotch collops, they even had a roast boar head as a centrepiece.

'Copied that from us,' Orvyn butted in, 'what about the rest of the body? You missed out on the best bits! Are you telling me you just threw away an entire boar, hocks and all?' Orvyn prodded the "would be" fire with his foot tutting and muttering away to himself about "ruddy royal folk".

Abigail went quiet. Des tried to lift the mood, comforting Abigail, who he had grown rather fond of, with the fact that he also ate turkey at Christmas.

'Lillian loved Christmas. She'd make a cracking roast and decorate the house all nice. Every year she'd make a new wreath for the front door.'

Orvyn let out a noise that was a mixture of extreme frustration and utmost ecstasy, much like one who reaches climax prematurely. 'Another thing we did! Stolen! Please tell me that you at least still set the wreath alight and roll it down a hill to entice Baldur to bring back the sun?'

'Not that I'm aware of, no.' Orvyn rolled his eyes at Des' response and if he had both arms intact, I'm sure they would've been firmly folded.

Des went on to speak of the *Vicar of Dibley*, outlining the Christmas episodes, specifically the one in which the vicar has to eat numerous Christmas dinners. Abigail found this most amusing, Orvyn, on the other hand, said that it would be more impressive if she had to eat several traditional pagan feasts. Abigail elbowed the Saxon. 'I'm sure you'd enjoy a Christmas dinner if you gave it a chance Orvyn. Come on.'

And so, the three friends paid homage to Dawn French's Geraldine Granger by walking around the entire village, going from meal to meal, leering in through dining room windows, where families and couples dined on everything from turkeys to nut roasts. Although they couldn't eat anything they sure as hell got as much enjoyment seeing the smiles on everyone's faces as crackers were pulled and jokes were told.

'What is that?' came Orvyn's voice, wrapped in wonderment.

They were peering in at a family of five, all sat round the table, eating away at what looked like the quintessential British Christmas dinner.

'What's what, Orvyn?' Des asked, his eyes still fixed on the pigs in blankets being served.

'That.' Looking across at him, Des could see that Orvyn was positively transfixed by—

'Gravy. Ovryn that is gravy.'

'Gravy? What is Gravy?' If Orvyn's salivary glands had been working, he'd look like a Neopolitan Mastiff watching his dinner be prepared.

'Think of it as meat juice. It's thick, warm and it tastes meaty. It's delicious.' Des was also now staring at the gravy boat lustfully.

'Hmmm meat juice,' moaned Orvyn, 'we had meat juice, but it wasn't like that. Perhaps some things change for the good.' Shockingly, that was the closest thing to a profound statement that Orvyn had ever or will ever utter.

Merry Christmas.

Chapter Eighteen
Thursday 1 January
New Year's Day

A week has passed since we were last with Des, Abigail and Orvyn. A couple of crucial things have happened since then, one being that Desmond Featherby had become accustomed to the reality that he will be forever in this plane of existence and that he might as well enjoy it as best he can, the other was Des' memorial. Reverend Daniels hiccoughed her way through a rather poorly attended service shortly after Christmas, following which Des' body was lowered into the ground next to his beloved Lillian. The headstone now reads:

Lillian Elizabeth Featherby
Born 4 August 1938
Died 19 October 2005
A loving wife and a loyal friend.

Desmond Edmund Featherby
Born 12 September 1930
Died 13 December 2014
A good husband and a great man.

Verity managed to get hold of Brian's eldest daughter, Grace, meaning that he was able to come and say farewell to his old friend. Des stood next to Brian during the lowering of his coffin, at one point Brian knelt down to tie up his laces and Des seized his opportunity for a bit of fun, pretending to rest his member on Brian's shoulder, making himself and Orvyn laugh. Des knew that Brian would also have found this highly comical. Des almost wished that someone would murder Brian right there and then just so they could spend more time together, but alas, Grace had assisted her father back into her Toyota Prius and they had silently and safely driven off, away from the village and away from Des. Henrietta and Lucy didn't stay for long either, they waited for Jarvis to have one final sniff around the hole into which his previous owner had just disappeared before they left. Verity stayed the longest, Annie hadn't even showed.

At the moment, it seems as though our tale is going to have a rather sorrowful ending with Des spending eternity in limbo and Chief Constable Wendy Mack getting off scot free, doesn't it?

You may be wondering, as I have, if there is actually any fathomable way for the ghosts in Orsworth to communicate with the living? The short answer is "no". The slightly longer answer is "no. Not quite yet". An answer of an appropriate length would be, 'No. Not quite yet... because the ghosts we have met thus far are all missing an absolutely necessary connection, none of them have a blood relative living in the village. The only way someone in the astral world can contact the living is if that person is a close relation. If they have that connection, they then possess the ability to visit their living relatives whilst they sleep, they can pass on any messages whilst their father, sister or indeed nephew is in dreamland.'

Woah wait a minute... "ghosts we have met *thus far*" that insinuates that we're going to be meeting another ghost before this tale ends. But there is only a page or so left, surely we're not going to have a left turn at this late stage in the game?

*

The ghosts that we've grown to know over the duration of this book were standing on the corner where Meadpath Street met the High Street. Des and Orvyn were doing their best to understand the rules of "Hot Cockles" for what felt like the ninety third time. Abigail was exasperated.

'What is so hard to understand? You sit down and close your eyes. We hit you and you have to guess who it was who hit you judging on the power and the angle!'

'And this is fun, is it?' said Des, raising his left eyebrow.

'Yes! My brothers and I used to play it all the time!' Abigail squealed with impatience.

'Were you always the one in the middle by any chance?' asked Des knowingly.

'I was yes, why does that matter?'

'No reason.' Des smiled

Abigail looked as though she was on the verge of giving herself a nervous breakdown when she noticed something that made her jaw drop.

'Oh my god.' She breathed. Des saw this sudden change in her and thought it best to placate Abigail. 'Okay, fine. We'll play Hot ruddy Cockles' – he sighed – 'Orvyn, you get in the middle.'

Orvyn jumped into the middle without question and closed his eyes. Abigail hadn't moved, her eyes were still locked onto something further down the road. Des looked at her and once his eyes had caught up with hers, his jaw dropped too.

'Is someone going to hit me or what?' said Orvyn who was now using his spare arm as a makeshift blindfold. When neither of the others responded, Orvyn opened his eyes and turned to them. 'Crikey Abi, you go on and on at us to play this game, and when we do finally say yes to it, you don't want to play. I mean, really, what is so impor—' Orvyn's jaw had dropped too.

Walking down the street, completely naked and utterly dead, was Annie.

Chapter Nineteen
Tuesday 27 January

Like a two pence piece tossed down a wishing well, a copper has gone down for good. Wendy Mack, ex Chief of Police has been arrested on three separate accounts, the murder of Annie Thorne, the murder of Desmond Featherby, and believe it or not, for the running of an illegal drug trade through the village bakery. Verity Thorne, Annie's mother, is to thank for bringing down the corrupt police officer. She said she was guided by the spirit of her recently deceased daughter, who came to her in her dreams, telling her what really happened, how Wendy Mack had beaten her to death with her own rolling pin, after Miss Thorne happened across Mack's journal. Her daughter also passed on messages from Mr Desmond Featherby who passed away late last year, insisting that Mack also killed him. Verity visited the station and spoke to an empathetic PC Bates, who went behind their chief's back to investigate her, even sneaking her gloves out of her coat pocket in the process. After two weeks of digging and several fibre reports, a special thank you to local forensic expert Peter Grosvenor, it was revealed that Mack had indeed killed Mr Featherby and had gone to the lengths of swapping and stealing his front door keys to pilfer back a drug filled carrot cake, which inadvertently led to PC Bates uncovering the drug trade which was being executed through Annie's bakery. The final person who came out against Wendy Mack was none other than the Kingpin of East Anglia himself, Malcolm Gibbs, who confessed that he had been working under Mack's instruction and guidance in return for protection. He assures and reassures the authorities and the press that he is now definitely out of that game, having finally set up a garden centre with his brother Iain.

Mack will be sentenced later this week, but we have a feeling that, like that two pence piece, she won't be coming back any time soon.

There was once a rumour that Warren's Walk was haunted by ghosts, now there is reason to believe that not just the woods but the whole of Orsworth is haunted, nay, not haunted, protected by these ghosts.

Extract from the *Orsworth Gazette*.

THE END